Acknowledgments

ALL MY THANKS TO MY GRACIOUS EDITORS,
KAREN WATSON AND RAMONA CRAMER TUCKER.

Abby—Quest for Treasure

SOUTH SEAS ADVENTURES

Abby
Quest
for Treasure

PAMELA WALLS

TYNDALE
KIDS

TYNDALE HOUSE PUBLISHERS, INC.
WHEATON, ILLINOIS

To June and Jime Crowe,
and Papa Clarke Harrisson,
thanks for your unconditional love!

Ask and it will be given to you; seek and you will find;
knock and the door will be opened to you.
Matthew 7:7

Chapter One
FEBRUARY 1848

Abigail Patience Kendall felt anything but patient.

Her teeth jarred each time Uncle Samuel's buckboard wagon hit a rut in the dirt road leading down the mountainside. Riding in the back among the empty baskets held only one benefit: She jostled next to Luke Quiggley, her fourteen-year-old best friend.

But Luke was snoozing in the noonday sun. With a mischievous flip of her wrist, Abby tossed her long hair off her shoulder and grinned with satisfaction when it struck him in the face.

"Hey!" Luke growled in mock anger.

She bit her lip to keep from smiling and looked innocently around at their surroundings. They'd been traveling a narrow dirt road surrounded by thick vegetation, where the Hawaiian trade winds couldn't reach them. But now the wagon began to lurch down the rock-strewn path toward an open spot on the mountainside.

Suddenly the cool breeze struck Abby in the face.

1

"Look!" Her cinnamon curls blew around her face as she pointed to the breathtaking view. "Our bay!"

Luke nodded at the sea. "Two ships are anchored off Kailua." As Luke and Abby drank in the beauty of turquoise water and white sandy beaches far below, a look passed between them. They remembered Captain Chandler's ship anchored there and the adventure that had brought them to Oahu.

The wagon descended on this steeper grade and began to pick up speed. "Whoa, Petunia!" Uncle Samuel roared. Abby saw him yank back on the reins as they veered closer to the cliff. She glanced at her younger sister sitting beside Uncle Samuel on the front seat. Little Sarah was clutching his arm with both hands. But there was no calming Petunia. The horse snorted in fright as the unexpected feel of the wagon harness pushed against her.

"The wagon's going too fast!" Abby screamed.

Luke bounced up and peered over the side. "We're just a few feet from the edge!" That edge, Abby knew, plunged one hundred feet to the beach!

"Whoa, girl," Uncle Samuel urged, "take it easy . . . you're doing fine." But the horse had been spooked, and the load gathered momentum on the downhill path. Suddenly a wheel dipped into a rut, flinging Abby against Luke. The wagon careened closer to the drop-off and teetered on the ledge.

"Move!" Luke gasped as he thrust Abby to the other side of the wagon. The horse whinnied in panic as the wheel pitched free of the hole, and the wagon jerked away from the cliff. Within seconds the road began to level out, and Uncle Samuel got Petunia under control.

Abby still gripped the side of the wagon with white knuckles. Her sunburned face had paled and her deep blue eyes were as wide as saucers. "Abby," Luke said, a smile tugging at his lips, "you can breathe again."

For an instant, she appeared startled. Then color flooded her face. "You . . . you rascal!" she shot back. For good measure, she whacked him playfully with the empty basket she'd brought along. "You know I hate heights!"

"It's okay to be scared," Luke said kindly. "See, I knew everything would be all right 'cause of *this*." As he dug into his pocket and pulled out his "lucky" white rabbit's foot on a chain, Abby groaned in frustration. But Luke gave her a teasing wink to let her know he didn't really mean it.

Or does he? Abby wondered. *When we faced danger a few months back, Luke prayed for the first time in years. But I haven't seen him talk to God since.* She had begun to worry about him again.

Then she remembered his quick actions to move her away from the ledge. Abby shook her head and gazed fondly at him. Who would have guessed when he moved to California more than three years ago that the lonely orphan boy from Pennsylvania would become her best friend?

The scent of *pikake* and plumeria trees rose in the heat along with the dust kicked up by the horse. As the path led away from the cliff and back through trees, Abby reached out and plucked two wide leaves from a banana tree. She held one out to Luke while shading herself with the other. "Forgot your bonnet again?" he asked, amusement on his tanned face.

"Yep." Abby stared at the back of eight-year-old Sarah's head. Even *she* had remembered her calico bonnet.

What I really want, Abby thought, *is a new tortoise comb to pile all this hair on top of my head. That would keep my neck cool.* But she knew there was no money for that. Not after hearing her parents' discussion last night. They had thought everyone was asleep, but the ranch-house walls were too thin to hide Pa's emotional words—words that kept returning to Abby.

"We're out of money, Charlotte!" Pa had said.

Then Ma's voice came through with quiet confidence. "The Lord will see us through, Thomas. He's never let us down."

"But it's never been this bad! At least in California we had our own vegetable garden. We've walked into a disaster! Samuel's been too sick to plant a garden or keep the cattle ranch going. It took all our money to get here. And there's no harvest, Charlotte! Do you know what that means?"

Abby had held her breath, waiting for Ma's answer: "We still have dried beans . . . and a little flour."

Pa's tortured tone had come through loud and clear. "How long will that last? I've got no money for more . . . and I doubt Samuel has, either."

4

Sarah's whine brought Abby back to the present. "Are we there yet?"

Uncle Samuel slapped the reins lightly against the mare's back and rubbed his shaggy beard. "Almost. See that hill?" He pointed ahead. "On the other side is Kailua and the mercantile your ma asked us to visit."

"What's at the mercantile, Uncle?" Abby asked. Sarah turned to gaze up into his face.

"Everything your heart could desire . . . cloth and food and leather goods. Last time I was in, I saw some white dishes with blue flowers on them." He clucked encouragement to the horse. "And there's ribbon candy that comes from Boston. Mmm . . . I love the peppermints. We'll have to see if there's any left."

Sarah jumped up and leaned forward. "Hurry up, Uncle! We gotta git us some of that candy before it's all gone!"

All gone, all gone . . . the money's all gone, Abby thought miserably. If Uncle Samuel had money, it should go for cornmeal and flour, like Ma had suggested. Not ribbon candy and tortoise combs. *Surely Uncle Samuel must have money if he's talking about candy. . . .*

When the wagon reached a rise in the dirt road, they began the last descent that led to the small town. Abby fanned herself with the banana leaf and hoped she'd see Olani, the Hawaiian chieftess who'd become her good friend. Entering Kailua, they passed the blacksmith shop and whitewashed church with the wooden cross on top. Soon Uncle Samuel's voice rang out, "Whoa, Petunia." He drew in the reins as he pulled up to the hitching post in front of the mercantile.

Abby and Luke scrambled out after Uncle Samuel, who held his arms up for Sarah. When she leapt into them gleefully, Abby cringed. *Poor Uncle Samuel!* Her father's older brother was as thin as a sapling since recovering from his illness. But he caught Sarah in midair and smiled at her enthusiasm.

"Let's go git us some candy!" Sarah urged, her slate blue eyes dancing with hope.

"Little Britches," Samuel said, "you and your family are just the medicine this poor old biologist needed to get well."

That's probably true, Abby thought as she retrieved the basket and they made their way into the dark interior of the little store.

When she'd first arrived at Uncle Samuel's ranch house, she'd been shocked. It wasn't only his haggard looks—he was an older version of Pa with a shaggy beard and long, pale-brown hair graying at the temples. But his house looked like a crowded storage shed, each bookshelf packed with birds' nests, dried flowers, rocks, and bugs in canning jars. Seashells, driftwood, and stuffed birds lined the kitchen cupboards where food supplies should have been. And Ma had already cleaned up some by the time Abby and Luke had finally arrived from their adventure of being lost at sea and getting tangled up in a mutiny.

Pa had immediately set to work building storage shelves so Ma could organize and start cooking for their thin uncle. Abby thought back fondly to the hours she and Luke had helped Uncle Samuel catalog and label the many Hawaiian artifacts he intended to save.

"Why's he need to label this stuff?" Luke had asked, amazed at the mess.

"Because he thinks someday it'll be important to have a record of it," Abby explained.

Just then Uncle Samuel had walked in and said, "That's right, young lady." He'd picked up an intricately carved paddle used by the Hawaiians on their canoe trips from island to island. "These wonderful people are dying out. The sailors and whalers from other nations have brought disease to paradise." He set down the paddle with a shake of his head. "Already, I'd say half of the Hawaiians are dead from it. Someday there will be even less of them. And when that happens, their way of life will disappear, too."

Abby's heart had stumbled at the thought. Not Olani and Kimo, her wonderful Hawaiian friends who'd helped her and Luke out of an awful jam! She thought of Olani, whose long, white hair made her look like the royalty she was. As bighearted as she was big-boned, Olani fondly called thirteen-year-old Abby a "little-bitty thing."

"Where's the candy?" Sarah asked, jolting Abby from her memory. Abby looked around the crowded store. Barrels of flour and sugar occupied much of the floor space, but tables of calico cloth, pots, pans, and dishes also jammed the place. Herbs, onions, and garlic braids hung from the ceiling, imported, she knew, from California. Horse saddles, leather boots, and Stetson hats adorned the back wall. But Uncle Samuel and Sarah were winding their way toward the counter, where large glass containers held bright ribbons of hard candy.

"I want the red and white ones!" Sarah beamed up at Uncle Samuel, as if he were her hero.

He smiled at the clerk. "How are you, Kipini?" Then he cocked his head at his little niece. "We need supplies—flour, cornmeal, and a few sweets."

The Hawaiian woman's round brown eyes crinkled in the corners with kindness. "*Aloha,* Samuel. Long time no see. You mo' better from sickness?" Her black hair was piled on top of her head with two tortoise combs, Abby noticed. And her dress, a full blue muumuu, looked cool and comfortable.

"Almost myself again," Uncle Samuel answered.

Abby came forward, peering longingly over her sister's white-blonde braid to the glass case that displayed brushes and tortoise combs. Kipini dragged a basket of ripe green apples across the top of the case toward Samuel and Sarah. "We get these apples two days ago from Oregon ship. Maybe you want some?"

Abby eyed the apples. "Oh, I could make a juicy pie for dinner!" Back in California she'd baked plenty of pies and fruit cobblers. She eagerly set her empty basket on the counter, her mouth almost watering with anticipation.

"Good idea." Samuel removed his money from his pocket, then noticed a paper sign hanging behind Kipini. "Flour prices have gone up?" he asked solemnly.

Something in Uncle Samuel's voice made Abby glance up. His lips were pursed, and he looked worried.

Kipini kept piling apples in the basket as she answered. "Prices go up, yes. We no get the shipload we expect. There is not so much to go around."

Uncle Samuel laid a hand on Kipini's to stop her. "I've decided against the apples for now. Let's concentrate on the flour and cornmeal."

Abby swallowed as Luke turned from the leather goods and gave her a questioning look. She shook her head sadly. *Uncle Samuel doesn't have money for apples!* Her heart picked up speed. If Ma and Pa didn't have money, and Uncle Samuel was almost out, what were they going to eat? His cattle were gone, and there was no crop to harvest. His last four chickens would eat better than anyone—they would always have a plentiful supply of bugs to eat in the barnyard! Abby dug her fingernails into her palms.

"I've never seen the righteous begging for bread," she'd heard Ma say. But Pa was right. *Things have never looked this bad,* Abby thought. *How is God going to supply now?*

Kipini scooped several pounds of flour into the center of a large banana leaf. She did the same with cornmeal, then wrapped each package snugly and put them in the basket. Pocketing the few coins Uncle Samuel offered, she selected two tart green apples and set them on top of the bundles. "I treat *kamali'i,* your children," she said with a serene expression.

Uncle Samuel rubbed his salt-and-pepper beard and cleared his throat. "Thank you kindly, Kipini." Then they headed out into the afternoon sunlight.

Luke and Abby climbed in the wagon while Samuel lifted Sarah onto the seat. "I'm sorry we couldn't get any candy, Little Britches."

"But we did! See?" Sarah opened her fist and revealed a long piece of red ribbon candy. "Enough for all of us." She began to break off pieces and hand them out. "Kipi-nini gave it to me." Abby and Luke giggled at Sarah's mangled version of *Kipini.*

Uncle Samuel chuckled and flapped the reins. The wagon jerked away from the mercantile as he murmured, "I love these people. . . . Their hearts are as big as the sea." Eyeing the sand dunes at the end of the dirt road, he suggested, "Why don't we stop by the water since we're already here?"

Luke whooped and Abby's face lit up. Sarah crunched her candy happily. Within five minutes,

Uncle Samuel drove the buckboard off the track and tied Petunia's reins to a low bush. The mare began eating leaves as the kids flew across the sugar-sand beach to the sparkling water. Tossing aside his shirt and boots, Luke dove into a breaking wave. Abby and Sarah hiked up their dresses to their knees and squealed with delight when the frothy wave swept over their legs and drenched their clothes. With each wash of seawater, the bubbles foaming into mermaid lace, Abby's concerns began to evaporate.

An hour later, after walking along the beach and gathering shells, they headed back to the wagon. Uncle Samuel had been telling them how no two shells were exactly alike. "Luke," Uncle Samuel asked as they got back to the wagon, "may I borrow your knife?"

"Sure." Luke fished it out of his shirt pocket and handed it over.

Samuel took one of the green apples and cut horizontally through it. "Look," he said, indicating the center. "What do you see?"

Sarah crowded in close. "There's a star inside!"

Abby glanced at her uncle, who loved to give lessons. "I didn't know the seeds were in the shape of a star."

He grinned at them. "You never know where you'll find stars," he continued. "Something special is hidden inside each of you, too."

"Hidden treasure?" Abby teased. Then her breath caught, for her words instantly reminded her of something—something so important, and yet she'd forgotten. . . .

"Exactly," Uncle Samuel explained. "The Lord put special talents in each one of you, talents that are like seeds waiting to bear fruit. Luke, Sarah, Abby," he addressed each one in turn, "you're each unique. I'll enjoy seeing what fruit your lives bear." Then he cut the apple in quarters and handed out the pieces.

The sweet-and-sour apple jolted Abby's tastebuds as an idea exploded in her mind. *Hidden treasure!* Why hadn't she thought of it before? She still had the treasure map from their previous voyage with Captain Chandler! It had been so easy to push the map to the back of her mind these past three months, enjoying the security of her family—and getting to know her sweet uncle again.

Why, maybe one of my hidden talents is treasure hunting, she thought. *Gold doubloons, silver dollars, jewels to grace Ma's lovely neck. . . .* Abby's eyes glistened. *If I find the treasure, I could solve my parents' problem!*

It was simple. All she had to do was follow the map she'd copied from Jackal, the blackhearted mutineer who'd caused them so much trouble on the way to Oahu. But at the thought of Jackal, her stomach tightened. Suddenly the gold was forgotten. The brawny pirate had promised to get even with her for dropping the original treasure map into the sea. She shivered, remembering the savage look on his face when he'd yelled, "I'll git ye!"

But he's in the stockade, the Honolulu prison, Abby reminded herself. *He can't get me. He can't.*

"Hop in, young 'uns," Uncle Samuel urged as he lifted Sarah high. He tugged Petunia away from the half-eaten bush. "Supper will be ready by the time we get home." Horse hoofs thudded softly on the dry dirt. As they passed through Kailua again, the air was filled with the sound of receding waves. Then they headed up the slope that led home.

All the while, Abby pondered her idea. The hidden treasure was just like that green apple: both sweet and tart. Sweet with the promise of wealth, and tart with the threat of unknown danger. Petunia plodded on the sunbaked earth, setting up a rhythm that pounded in Abby's mind. *Should I go?* she asked herself over and over. *Can I really find a hidden treasure that will change our lives?*

Chapter Two

As the wagon drove into the clearing where the ranch house was located, Uncle Samuel sat up stiffly. "Blazes!"

"What is it, Uncle Samuel?" Abby asked, stunned by his outburst. She followed his gaze to the front porch, where a large black stallion was tied.

Uncle Samuel slapped the reins impatiently against Petunia's hindquarters, and she broke into a fast trot. "Boris Rassmassen, that's what!" Abby had heard the name before. He was an overseer at a nearby ranch.

At the porch steps, Samuel reined in the horse. "Luke, take care of the wagon," he ordered as he leapt off the seat and started up the porch stairs. He almost ran into a tall, muscular man who was just emerging through the door. In a flash, Abby noted the difference between skinny Uncle Samuel's features and Rassmassen's wide chest, heavy work boots, and commanding presence.

"How nice to see you, Samuel." The man spoke

with a German accent. But from the way his lips curled into a snarl, Abby knew he hadn't meant the words. She climbed from the wagon in time to see anger spreading across Uncle Samuel's face.

"Rassmassen, what do you want?" Uncle Samuel stood his ground on the porch.

"Just came to make a friendly call, ja? Met da fraulein, Mrs. Kendall. She offered me tea. I'm sure if she'd had da supplies, she would have offered more." The man set his widely brimmed hat on his head and stared arrogantly at Uncle Samuel. "But I know you've had troubles, Samuel."

Rassmassen swept his hand around the yard, the corral empty except for four chickens scratching in the dirt. "Obviously, da ranch isn't producing. Maybe if you hadn't spent the last few years collecting birds' nests . . ." He cackled at his own brand of humor, then sobered. "But dese tings have a way of righting demselves."

"What do you mean?" Uncle Samuel sounded wary.

"What I mean is, dis place will become profitable—after I buy it."

Samuel exploded. "This is *my* place! You can't do that!"

"Oh, I can—and you know it. All dis belongs to the king, and he could take it back anytime he wanted." Abby found his calm voice unnerving, as if he feared nothing . . . as if Rassmassen were used to getting his way.

"But now, with dis Great Mahele," he continued, "anyone can buy property from da king and receive permanent ownership papers." Rassmassen's large hand strayed to his hip and rested on the hilt of a whip that hung from his belt.

Samuel's eyes narrowed as he took an aggressive step toward the larger man. "Why, you dirty, low-down, swindling . . ."

Suddenly, Pa barrelled through the front door. He gripped his brother by the arm and shoved him out of Rassmassen's way. "Let the man by, Samuel. There's no sense discussing it." Abby saw Pa's face tighten and his jaw clench.

Rassmassen smirked and walked lightly down the steps, the whip bouncing against his hip. "Good day, gents," he said as he brushed by Abby as if she weren't there and mounted his horse. The leather creaked under his weight as he jerked the dark stallion around and spurred it into a gallop.

Uncle Samuel broke loose from Pa and stormed to the other side of the porch. "The man's a cheat! Everyone knows it. Last year he stole Josiah Winston's sugar profits in a dirty game of cards. And I've seen the bloody backs he's given some field-workers. . . . I don't like him!"

Pa stalked over to his brother. "I don't like him either, Samuel. But he intends to take your ranch. We've got to find a way to get that money—before he does." Abby watched in horror as Pa sank down onto the porch railing and rested his head on his hands. The image of Pa's hopelessness burned into her mind.

Just then Ma bustled out to the porch. "It's time for you children to come inside and wash up for dinner." She hurried Sarah and Abby through the door and shut it behind her. "Your pa needs to talk with Samuel alone," she explained. "And you need to set the table." The girls followed her toward the kitchen.

Looking out the front room's one window, Abby saw Luke leading the horse into the barn. Then she turned back to the kitchen. After washing her hands in a bucket, she picked up a stack of dinner plates and took them to the table. Ma and Sarah were setting out the forks and knives.

Abby only heard snippets of their conversation. "Ma," Sarah said in a tattletale tone, "Abby forgot her sunbonnet again today. She's gonna git more freckles. . . ."

"Shush, Sarah. It's not nice to tell . . ." Abby didn't hear the rest. Her mind was far away. Her heart was thrumming wildly as she wrestled with a decision.

It's up to me. Rassmassen will steal our home unless I get that gold. I've got to leave soon. Then she corrected herself. *We've got to leave soon.* Certainly Luke would be eager for adventure. But she swallowed hard. *Can I do it, God? It will take hours of hiking to search for the treasure. Will my legs make it? Even from our short walk today, my legs are tired. If only I didn't have Ma's weak legs!* she lamented. *But I have no choice.*

The evening meal was quiet. Abby washed up the dinner dishes and Luke dried while Ma kneaded bread dough on the kitchen table with an unusual zeal. *Maybe Ma's imagining it's Boris Rassmassen's face,* thought Abby.

The front door of the ranch house stood open, drawing moths to the lantern that lit the room. A cool breeze wafted in and rustled the outside trees, giving them soft music to work by.

"Luke," Abby whispered as she handed him another chipped plate, "we've got to talk later tonight and make important plans."

"What plans?" His eyebrows shot up in question.

Abby nodded at her mother, who had punched down her loaf for the last time and was setting it in the bread pan to rise. "Shhh . . ."

Luke's green eyes sparkled. "A secret?"

"What'd you say, Luke?" Ma eyed them as she carried the pan to the stove.

Abby and Luke exchanged glances. "We were discussing plans for the night, Ma. Do you . . . do you think we could get Uncle Samuel to play his guitar again?"

Ma wiped her floured hands on her apron. "I'm sure he could be coaxed. It'd be especially good to hear music tonight." She pushed a hairpin in at the nape of her neck and untied her apron. "After I trim his hair, we can sit outside where the breeze can reach us."

"Great idea." Abby dried her hands on the kitchen towel and grabbed Luke's hand as he set down the last dish. "Come on." They hurried out the door in search of her uncle, who was just returning from the barn with Sarah on his shoulders.

"Uncle Samuel, would you play your guitar for us tonight?" Abby hoped he'd give in. Ever since the afternoon, her mind had been buzzing with questions about Lanai, the site of the buried treasure. But she didn't know much about the distant island . . . only that it lay close to Maui.

"It's about time we lightened the mood," Uncle Samuel answered. "But your ma promised to shear some of this sheep's wool off my head. First things first." He scrubbed his salt-and-pepper beard absently. "As soon as that's done, we'll have a serenade. Luke and Abby, why don't you build a fire pit and we'll sing under the stars?"

Everyone scattered to hurry the evening along. By the time Abby and Luke returned from the woodpile and began building a fire, Ma, Sarah, and Pa were watching Uncle Samuel lather up his bearded face on the front porch. Uncle Samuel stared into a mirror that dangled from one of the wooden posts.

"Now, Charlotte," he said, "I don't want to look like a newborn lamb. Just a trim'll do."

Ma wagged her finger at him. "Samuel, you look like a shaggy wolf. I'm going to make you presentable to society again."

Uncle Samuel winced, but Ma didn't back down. "Sit here and I'll try to perform a minor miracle."

Sarah perched on the porch railing and patted his shoulder for support. "I'm right here, Uncle. Don't be scared."

"You'll love me no matter what I look like?" he asked his younger niece.

Sarah placed her palm on his lathered whiskers. "Always," she said solemnly, her blue eyes round and kind. She wiped off the lather on Samuel's dusty shirt.

Abby and Luke gathered round as Pa sharpened the straight-edge razor on a leather strap. When finished, he handed the shiny instrument to Ma, who took it and tilted Samuel's head back. "Don't move, Samuel, or I could take off more than I mean to."

In a few short minutes, Ma had whisked away Uncle Samuel's beard, but she'd left muttonchop whiskers. Then she took up her sewing shears and began to trim the unkempt hair hanging over his ears and collar. "I declare, Samuel, you might look like a scientist yet," she said brightly as she removed the rag he'd tied around his neck. "Go wash and let's see what we've done."

Uncle Samuel hurried away to the horse trough

and dunked his whole head in. "It feels good, Charlotte! Half-a-year's growth gone!" When he tromped back, dripping wet, Ma dried him off with a towel and combed his hair, parting it properly down the side.

"Take a gander in the mirror and tell me how you like it," she urged.

Uncle Samuel whistled into the dim glass. "I do clean up nice, don't I?"

He was teasing them, Abby knew, so she went over to curtsy in front of him. "Oh, kind and handsome sir, may I have this waltz?" Sarah giggled from the sidelines as Uncle Samuel gallantly swept Abby into a waltz, to music he began to hum. After Sarah and Abby had each taken a turn around the porch, they all headed down to the blazing fire. Pa had spread out burlap sacks to sit on, and each found a spot. Abby sat next to Uncle Samuel and across the pit from Luke.

When Samuel picked up his battered guitar, everyone hushed expectantly. Then he began strumming a lively tune about a Molokai princess who "loved the son of a sailor man." As they clapped to the rousing beat, the evening flew by. Soon the fire began to burn low. Sarah snuggled sleepily in Pa's arms, which meant the night was drawing to a close. But Abby had not yet gotten the answers she sought. "Uncle Samuel, you've lived a long time in the Sandwich Islands," Abby began. "Have you ever been to the island of Lanai?"

Uncle Samuel turned toward her, surprised. As he looked into her eyes, Abby held her breath. Did he suspect her plans?

"I've never been there myself," he finally said, "but I've talked to folks who've visited. The name *Lanai* means 'day of conquest.' " He rubbed his smooth chin. "It's aptly named. Some say the island is haunted."

Luke sat up from where he'd been listening intently. "Haunted?" he echoed.

"Yes, seventy years ago the island people were murdered by warriors from 'the Big Island.' No one survived the massacre. Some say Lanai is haunted by the ghosts of those who were never properly laid to rest." Goose bumps instantly rose up Abby's arms, and the night turned eerie.

"Do you know how the Hawaiians bury their dead?" Uncle Samuel asked.

Abby could see the lecture coming. Heading it off, she asked, "Do *you* think it's haunted, Uncle Samuel?"

"As a Christian, I don't have to worry about those things," Uncle Samuel said confidently. "Greater is He who is in me than he who is in the world." He patted Abby on the back and smiled. "Why this sudden interest in Lanai, the tiny red island?"

"Ah, well . . ." Abby's gaze veered to Luke, hoping he'd come to her rescue, but it was Pa who sighed and rose to his feet with Sarah asleep in his arms.

"Enough chatter for now." He turned to Samuel. "We've got to rise early if we want to hunt wild pigs and bring home the bacon. It's time we all get to bed." Sarah sighed and tucked her head under Pa's chin. Pa nuzzled her. "Luke, would you knock down the fire so we don't have to worry about flying sparks?"

"Yessir." Luke jumped up and reached for a stick.

"I'll collect the burlap sacks, Pa, then be right to bed," Abby volunteered.

Ma came over and gave Abby a hug. "Come to bed soon, love. There's book-work in the morning. We can't let our lessons fall behind just because we live far from civilization." Ma and Uncle Samuel followed Pa. Abby waited for their boots to sound on the porch steps before she moved toward Luke.

"It's time," Abby announced breathlessly.

"For bed?" he asked, brushing a lock off his forehead.

"No, you goose. It's time to go after the buried treasure—you know, the map!"

He shot her a knowing look. "So that's why you were asking about Lanai. I thought you'd forgotten about it." For a second, she saw excitement blaze in his eyes. But then he sobered and bent to stir the campfire.

Abby picked up a burlap sack. "I-I did. I didn't . . . want to leave. But my parents need that treasure— and Uncle Samuel needs to buy the ranch before that wicked Rassmassen does." The firelight danced across her face. "Luke, they're out of money!"

Luke grimaced, then stared out into the dark kukui forest.

"What?" Abby demanded. "Are you afraid 'cause Lanai's supposedly haunted?"

Luke snorted. "No! I know God helped us last time. But I don't want to put your parents through more worry. It was *my* fault they thought you were lost at sea. I'm not eager to give them a reason to . . ." Finally he pushed a hand through his straight hair and said bluntly, "I'm trying to make myself useful around here."

"Luke, my parents love you. You don't have to earn that."

"I know! But if my aunt writes, it's gonna be hard for them to keep me here." He sighed heavily. "I've been expecting a letter all month."

Abby saw sadness in his eyes, and her heart softened. "But don't you see? If we get that gold, we'll save the ranch. You can't get any more useful than that." She took his cold hand in hers. "I've got it all figured out. We'll catch a ride to Maui—maybe Olani knows a sea captain in Kailua who can help us. From Maui we can get a ride to Lanai. . . . Then we follow the map. We'll only be gone two weeks. What could go wrong?"

Luke stared at her, openmouthed. "We could get caught in another mutiny!"

"That's not likely!" she shot back. Then, seeing

Luke wasn't convinced, she squeezed his hand.
"Luke, we've *got* to get that money before
Rassmassen takes our ranch."

"I know," he said, resigned. "I want to help. . . .
Eating three meals a day makes me feel guilty. And
I'm always hungry!" He exhaled and threw down
his stick. "All right, we'll go. How soon do you want
to leave?"

"How about tonight?"

"Tonight?" Luke wrinkled his face in distaste.
"Don't you think it'd be better to get a good start in
the morning, after breakfast? Your ma's gonna have
bread baking at sunrise."

She shook her head. "I know you love warm
bread, but we'll bring crackers and some of those
hard-boiled eggs. I have a few cents I brought from
California—just enough for bread. Once we get the
gold, we'll buy all the supplies we need: more chickens, apples, and lots of ribbon candy!" She grinned
at him. "But one thing's for sure; we've got to be
gone before Pa rises to go hunting."

Luke crossed his arms. "I'm not going unless you
leave a note. . . . I don't want your parents worrying
again."

"It's a deal," she said, holding out her hand to
him. When they shook, Abby sighed with relief.
Luke was coming with her! Together they could
accomplish anything. And it wouldn't be long
before they returned with enough money—gold!—
for everything they needed.

"I'll tap on your window in about four hours," he said, as he headed toward his bunk in the barn, where he'd transformed the tack room into his own private place.

"Thanks." Abby picked up the last burlap sack and started for the ranch house. She was already imagining Uncle Samuel unfurling a deed of ownership in Boris Rassmassen's unpleasant face. The man would stomp away, angry—and defeated! *Sweet Uncle Samuel will never have to worry again,* she thought as she climbed the porch steps.

Setting down the burlap sacks, she imagined Pa's eyes bugging out when she and Luke lugged home a chest of gold. They'd set it right here on the porch. Then Pa would grab her in a victory hug and gaze down at her with pride shining in his blue eyes. As she headed toward the straw-tick mattress she and Sarah shared, Abby realized a weight had lifted from her heart. Snuggling next to her sister, she closed her eyes and thought, *This is going to work out perfectly!*

Chapter Three

A day and a half later, Abby took a steadying breath. They had made it to the island of Maui. An ocean breeze blew across Lahaina, gently rocking ships at anchor. Sunshine glinted off the sea ripples and shimmered like a thousand silver fish scales. But in spite of Maui's island beauty, Abby's pulse quickened as she watched the shadow of a large man slip around the corner of the Pioneer Inn. *Now I'm sure.*

She leaned toward Luke. "He's been following us since we started wandering through town, looking for lunch." This was the third time she'd seen the man since they'd sailed into Lahaina Harbor. Olani's friend, a sea captain, had given them free passage. But each time Abby spied the strange man tailing them, he hid himself.

"Luke!" Abby hissed. He made no response but sat propped, eyes closed, against the trunk of a banyan tree set in a square near the inn and harbor. They'd just bought and eaten several cents' worth of stale bread from a bakery. Apparently, Luke's full belly had lulled him to sleep.

Abby scowled at him. This was no time to sleep, even though they'd had little of it since leaving her uncle's ranch in the middle of the night.

"Wake up, lazybones! There's trouble afoot."

The word *trouble* instantly conjured up in Abby's mind a picture of Pa. She gulped. After a day of thinking about it, she'd begun to worry that Pa might not take kindly to her leaving home without his permission—even if it was for the family. So she just had to find that treasure! She couldn't face Pa unless she returned with a chest of gold.

But already they'd hit a snag. Who was that man following them?

Beginning to feel desperate, Abby grabbed Luke's muslin shirt under his chin and tugged. He opened one bloodshot eye. "What?"

"We're being followed! We've got to get out of here," she said urgently.

Luke's other eye creaked open. "Abby, no one here even knows we have a treasure map."

"What if that man's an escaped sailor from the *Flying Lady*—out to follow us and steal the gold?"

Luke sat up straight, concern finally registering. He seemed to study the area. But all he could see were a few sailors sitting near the wharf mending nets. Nothing looked out of the ordinary. "I don't see anyone," he said in a puzzled tone.

"Every time I spy him, he disappears," Abby said, worried.

"You're spooking easily. The mutineers are locked up at the fort in Honolulu. They can't get us, Abby." Luke leaned toward her, his silky-straight hair tumbling across his forehead. "This *should* be fun, Ab . . . as long as we don't jump before we think—like last time." He gave her upturned nose a playful tweak.

Abby bit her bottom lip. "It was quick thinking that got us the treasure map," she reminded him.

"I admit your drawing comes in handy now and then. But Abigail *Patience* Kendall—you're too impulsive. Too bad your parents didn't wait to get to know you before they named you!" Luke's cheeks dimpled. "I'd say your parents were downright impulsive naming you!"

Abby yanked her calico sunbonnet off her shoulders and set it back on her head. This time, for once, she'd remembered to bring it. "Well, I'm going to *impulsively* get a move-on." Her eyes blazed briefly. "When you're grabbed from behind, just remember—I warned you!" She jumped up and headed toward the water, her blue calico dress flouncing like a wave-splash around her ankles and high-button boots.

Luke sighed and stood. Grabbing their pack, he hurried after her. "Don't get a bee in your bonnet," he hollered, following.

Abby, who had almost reached the harbor, waited for him to catch up.

"All right," he asked, "what'd this villain look like?"

Glad Luke was finally taking her seriously, she smiled up at him under the noonday sun. "He's tall, wears a hat pulled down low, a pale yellow shirt, brown vest . . . oh, yes, and a patch over his left eye," she said.

"You sure he's not sporting a peg leg and a gold earring, too?" Luke teased.

Abby gripped the ribbons of her sunbonnet and tied them securely under her chin. "You think I'm making this up?" she said, stomping away, too annoyed to notice the horse droppings in her path until it was too late. "Ugh! Look what you made me do!" Stepping gingerly to a patch of weeds, she wiped off her boot.

Luke scrunched his nose at the scent wafting upward in the hot sun. "Don't get your crinoline in a twist. It's just hard to believe there's a convict following us on a beautiful day like this."

Abby's nostrils flared as she took a deep breath. "After all we've been through, Luke Quiggley, I never thought I'd see the day you doubted me. That man *is* following us, and he *does* look like a villain, like a varmint, like . . ." She trailed off in exasperation, about to storm toward the water when her eyes widened. "Just like *him!*" she said, pointing over Luke's shoulder.

The fear in Abby's eyes made Luke turn quickly.

They both saw a man stepping behind the banyan tree they'd just left. But he hadn't been as fast as Abby's eagle eyes.

Luke grabbed Abby's left arm with his free hand and tugged. "Come on! We'll move toward the dock and try to lose him."

Abby scanned the rickety dock as she stumbled along next to Luke. "I don't see anywhere to hide!" There were no buildings, only several barrels recently unloaded by four men in a rowboat.

"Hurry," Luke urged as their boots made hollow thumps on the wooden dock boards. They could see the green harbor water between the slats. "Behind those barrels."

Before she and Luke hid behind them, Abby glanced back at the banyan tree. But she couldn't see their pursuer.

"I'm sorry, Abby," Luke said, his eyes softening. "You were right."

"Hey! What're ye kids doin'?" A burly sailor, dressed in dirty duck cloth, stood up in a rocking dory and glared at them. Three other sailors were in the boat with him.

Luke gulped. "Just resting, sir." As the sailor eyed them suspiciously, Abby realized he could give away their hiding spot. She had to put an end to the conversation.

"We're looking for a ship that can take us to Lanai."

"Oh, and why might that be?" the sailor asked curiously.

Abby tried to sound both casual and in control. "We have business there."

The sailor continued winding the hemp rope into a coil, then dropped it in the bottom of the rocking boat. "We go right by Lanai this afternoon. I'll ask me cap'n."

He pushed off from the wharf and, as he and his three companions pulled on the oars, the rowboat skittered toward the harbor entrance. They were heading to one of the many ships at anchor off Lahaina, home to the Pacific whaling fleet.

Abby remembered Uncle Samuel's words: "These waters lie in the protective shelter of four islands— Maui, Lanai, Molokai, and Kahoolawe." This calm sea had become known around the world as a safe place to harbor, so each year more ships stopped. They brought rowdy sailors looking for whiskey and a rollicking good time.

"Abby," Luke said, annoyed, "we don't even know those men. Sometimes you're like a cricket that jumps through an open window—never knowing what's on the other side. It could be a cat, waiting for a meal!" With a sound of exasperation, Luke watched the jollyboat skim over the dark blue water. "How do you know it's safe to get a ride to Lanai with those sailors?"

"Ah, actually I don't," Abby admitted, knowing she *had* been a bit hasty. "But we do need a ride and now seemed like a good time to get one." She brushed her flying hair out of her face as the breeze swept in from the sea.

"Right out of the frying griddle and back into the fire," he muttered.

"Luke," Abby began, remembering the mutiny they'd endured during their last sailing adventure, "what are the chances lightning strikes twice in the same place? Ah . . . or on the same people?"

"I guess we're already in the fire if that big man really is trailing us. One thing's for sure . . . life with you is never boring—Cricket."

Abby stuck her tongue out at him. "I don't like being called a bug. But nothing can be as bad as last time." She shook her head as if to free herself from the bad memories of Jackal.

They settled back against two barrels to wait for the return of the burly sailor. Abby watched as the rowboat arrived at a schooner that looked as if it had seen better days. It appeared theirs was a small crew, which worked rapidly at lowering more cargo. Within minutes the sailor and his companions rowed back to the dock, their dory laden with more barrels. When they finished unloading, the sailor squinted at Abby, as if sizing her up.

"Cap'n says yer welcome to a free ride to Lanai, since we're goin' right by Kamaiki Point. But if ye want to go any farther, ye better have money to pay passage."

"Lanai is as far as we need to go," Abby said, her heart tripping with excitement. She'd found them a ride only hours after landing in Lahaina! "And thanks," she added to the sailor as Luke helped her into the bobbing boat. Luke tossed her their one satchel and then jumped in after her, throwing the dory into a fit of rocking. When they were seated, he said softly, "You promised you wouldn't jump into anything, remember?"

She elbowed him in the ribs. "I'm sure this will work out. The captain's probably as nice as Captain Chandler. Besides, it's not like we're carrying money or anything valuable." Then she remembered the treasure map. "Oops."

As they rowed out of the harbor, the sailors talked among themselves as if the kids weren't there. Abby and Luke sat forward, face into the wind, eyes on the distant island of Lanai, a mere nine sea miles away. They would be there before nightfall! She gave Luke a satisfied grin. "About time an adventure went our way."

The men heaved into the oars, their strokes taking them out of the harbor and into sea swells that rocked the boat and threw spray over everyone.

Abby loved the ocean and smiled when the salt spray jetted into her eyes. But the joy left her face as she realized the sailors were talking about recent events on Oahu. As the men burst into laughter, she struggled to hear the burly sailor's words. ". . . The pirate weren't in the stockade more'n two months before he escaped."

As the dory drew closer to the ancient ship,

Luke's eyes were bright with the unspoken question: *Who were they talking about?*

Another sailor grunted as he pulled his oar. "If ye ask me, he musta bribed a guard. No one gets out of prison that easy."

Abby's stomach clenched into a knot as she peered at Luke. He, too, appeared shaken, for a muscle twitched at his jaw. "Who are you gentlemen talking about?" he asked the sailors.

"Ah, some mutineer that got caught off Oahu. I saw the poster of him up at the mercantile. He's a mangy-looking beast, all right. Got teeth like the tusks on a wild boar."

Abby's heart hammered, and blood roared in her ears. She moved closer to Luke on the bench. "He wouldn't happen to have a very black beard, would he?" she asked.

The sailor spoke with genuine surprise. "How'd ye know?"

But the first sailor interrupted with a cackle. "I hear he goes by the name of Jackal. What self-respectin' man would keep a name like that, I ask ye?"

The two kids blanched at the name.

"Maybe he's proud of it," another sailor jeered. "Or maybe his momma give it to him!" The group of sailors guffawed as they rowed one last time to draw alongside the decrepit ship that was taking Abby and Luke to Lanai.

Three of the men ran nimbly up the ship's rope ladder while one stayed below and held it, keeping the rowboat in place. Abby glanced at the peeling black paint on the ship's side and almost chuckled when she read the name *Beauty* in fading white letters. She hiked the hem of her skirt and tried to fit her foot into the first rung, but the chop moved the dory. It heaved up, then back down again, and she moved out of reach of the ladder. On the next surge up, she gripped the ladder with both hands, thankful Luke had their satchel and the hidden treasure map. Then she clambered up the swinging ladder.

It was then the memory hit her: Abby's hands became clammy as she vividly recalled climbing up Captain Chandler's ladder. Jackal was already onboard and had lunged at her as she dropped his precious treasure map into the sea. His lip had curled back in a snarl of hatred, and she'd heard the curse on his lips, "I'll git ye!"

Abby's breath caught. If Jackal was free, not only was the treasure in jeopardy . . . so were their lives!

Climbing over the railing, she reached a trembling hand down for the satchel, then looked back toward shore as Luke ascended.

"Oh, no," she cried as he clambered aboard and took the baggage from her.

"What now?" he asked. But Abby only gazed in stunned silence. Luke followed her eyes to the dock they'd just left. There, standing beside the barrels at the end of the wharf, was a huge man who was lowering a small telescope from his eye.

His other eye was hidden by a black patch.

Chapter Four

"Ho, there, girlie." The words flew across the narrow deck. Abby turned in surprise as a heavyset man with a bulging stomach strode toward her on bowed legs. He wore the same dirty work clothes of the other sailors but walked with a swagger, as if he were in charge. One front tooth was missing, and his thinning gray hair had receded to the top of his head. He smelled of garlic and sweat.

"Hold there, passengers. I be the cap'n of this grand vessel, the *Beauty*," he said with a sly smile. "The name is Cap'n Jim." He stuck out a calloused hand, which was tanned from the sun but covered with white warts.

Abby had immediate reservations about the man but shook his hand anyway. "Thank you for the ride, Captain Jim."

Luke also stuck out a hand and greeted the grimy man. Cap'n Jim's gum showed when he responded. "Always glad to do a good turn. In fact, we'll be comin' back by Lanai in ten days' time and can pick ye up again. But tell me, as we get underway—"he paused and moved to give a sailor room to haul up a sheet—"all about yer business there." Men were busy everywhere, and Abby could hear the grinding creak of the anchor being raised.

She swallowed hard when she saw the look in the captain's eyes: It was greed, plain and simple. Slanting a glance at Luke, she could tell he'd caught it, too.

"Captain," Luke began, "I hope you'll excuse us for not discussing it. You see, we're doing a good deed for Abby's parents, but we're sworn to secrecy."

The captain rubbed his grizzly chin and looked at them with narrowed eyes. "Hmm. I can't imagine what business ye could be havin' on that spit-dry island . . . no natives live there. But perhaps I see more than ye think I do."

He took out a tin of tobacco and put a chaw of it inside his lip. He scowled out over the water toward the small island in the distance, as if seeing something far away or long ago. "In all me years of sailin' through these beauteous islands, I've only taken passengers to Lanai a few times," he said thoughtfully.

Suddenly the spell seemed to break and he brightened. "No difference. Stay out of the way of me men, and ye shall have yer free ride to Lanai. There be no help for ye there. But smart people like yerselves would know that already. Am I right?" He cocked an arrogant eyebrow at Luke, who shrugged but didn't look too pleased.

"We don't know as much about Lanai as we'd like, Captain," Abby said, glad they'd sidestepped a potential problem. Captain Jim was the last person with whom she wanted to share information about hidden treasure. "Could you tell us more?" She clung to the wooden boom overhead and smiled at him.

"Not much to tell, missy. Yonder island is a desolate place. Some say the island is haunted. I've heard tell it's inhabited by the spirits of those who were murdered there. . . . I know of one meself."

Abby's stomach curled uncomfortably. Luke stared incredulously at the captain.

"Sometimes, when I'm anchored in Lahaina Roads, I can see fires blinkin' on Lanai. Can't figure it. Maybe ye will discover what causes those lights and tell me. . . . if we ever meet again." The captain rubbed his beard stubble absently and glanced back toward Lanai. "Besides, it's a dry island—hard to find water. But surely ye come prepared for it." With that, he scuttled off like an oversized crab to oversee his crew.

"Luke," Abby said, her blue eyes startled, "we haven't come prepared! We don't have any water with us!"

Luke grimaced; they were already under sail. "I don't think there's any going back now, Ab. The captain's not going to turn the ship around. But maybe he'll give us a jug of water to take with us 'til he returns in ten days' time to pick us up."

"I hope so," Abby fretted. Ten days was a long

time. She'd wanted this to be a clean and tidy adventure . . . no nasty surprises like last time when mutineers had almost sold her and Luke as slaves to China. She just wanted to get to Lanai, find the treasure, and go home. A sense of urgency nagged her, as if maybe she shouldn't have come.

"Let's keep a look out for dolphins," Luke suggested. "We've got some time ahead of us."

They settled down to watch the flying fish dart out of the ship's way as they headed straight toward the mountain of Lanai. Abby rummaged through their bag and pulled out a handkerchief. She unwrapped the white bandana and offered a crumbling biscuit to Luke. They'd loaded up on stale goods from the Lahaina bakery, thinking they could live off Lanai's fruit until they returned with the gold.

Luke took one crumbling biscuit with a grin. "I'm starving."

She laughed. "You're always starving." But she knew they hadn't had a full meal in a day. "I was hoping we'd find friendly natives on Lanai, like we did on Maui. But I guess we'll have to scout for papaya and coconuts ourselves when we get there."

Luke nodded. "Let's hope we find fruit—and fresh water." He wiped the crumbs from his mouth. "Hey, why don't we stay out of the way at the bow?"

They headed forward and watched, chin on hands, as the water roared by. Sunlight streamed down into the deep sea channel, setting aflame flecks of gold and silver in the dark blue water.

Flying fish startled Abby and thrilled her as they leapt out of the water and sailed above the waves with fins that beat as fast as hummingbird wings.

Once Abby sighted a white plume of vapor far off. She heard a sailor call, "Whale to starboard!" In these waters, however, most of the leviathans had been so hunted that they fled from ships. So the white plume soon disappeared.

The wind pumped the sails full and drove them through the Auau Channel in record time. It was a calm, uneventful ride for almost three hours as the sailors onboard paid them no mind. Pretty soon, Abby could see the shoreline of Lanai. A curved, white sandy bay beckoned, but the island certainly did look deserted.

The burly sailor came forward. "Time for you kids to get off," he shouted into the headwind.

Abby shook Luke, who had fallen asleep. "Time to rise and shine," she said excitedly. "We're here, safe and sound!"

The two made their way to the captain, who stood eyeing the pale shoreline. "Manele Bay," he said, pointing to the arc of dazzling sand surrounded by green vegetation. They were sailing west, but the island's southwestern cliffs shaded them from the sun's light. The day was drawing to a close. "We're beyond Kamaiki Point, but this spot will suit ye better."

"Captain," Abby began tentatively, "would you

please loan us the use of a jug . . . ah, filled with fresh water?"

"Ye didn't plan well, did ye?" Captain Jim chortled in an unnerving way, showing off his missing front tooth. "Lucky for ye, I did! I be droppin' ye off where there's a fresh stream that enters the bay there," he said pointing.

"Oh, how nice," Abby said. "But could we still take a jug to carry water with us?"

The captain nodded to his burly sailor, who went below and returned a minute later with a pickle crock stoppered with a cork. "Sure, and I'm a thoughtful man," said the captain smugly. "Now it's over the side with ye. Time to swim to shore!"

Abby started to grin. He had to be jesting! They were a hundred yards from shore. But the captain wasn't smiling. Luke glanced at the shore and back to the captain again.

Thunderstruck, Luke asked, "Captain, you're joshing us?"

"Jump and swim," the captain bellowed angrily. "We be pushin' on to Oahu. If ye be goin' on with us, there's passage to pay!"

"But our food—our bag—will be ruined," Abby objected.

The captain handed her a cork life ring with a rope attached. "Tie yer victuals to this," he advised. "But ye've got only seconds, missy, before the wind carries us on." Several of the crew had stopped working to watch the unfolding drama. Abby's eyes fixed on the desolate shore, then swung back to the deep blue sea. She remembered the last time she'd gone overboard; she'd had a close brush with a shark! The shadows on the sea frightened her.

But Luke moved forward and began climbing over the ship's railing.

"Abby, we've got to jump," Luke said, taking the cork ring from her hand and loosely tying the satchel to it. He flung it into the sea, where the satchel bobbed on the chop.

"Come on," he ordered and held out his free hand to her. Abby gripped it and climbed over the railing, balancing carefully in her high-button boots and long dress.

"At least we've got the life ring," she said just as Luke jumped away from the sailing ship, pulling Abby through the air with him.

Chapter Five

Abby smacked the water and submerged, her boots
filling and her dress and undergarments clinging.
When Luke let go of her hand, a wave hit her in the
face. Panic gripped her in the chest as she fought to
keep her head above water.

"Luke!" she gasped. In seconds he was back beside
her, hauling the satchel and life ring with him.

"Hold this, Abby!" He tread water while she
grabbed the cork ring and felt it buoy her up some.
They both watched as the *Beauty* moved past them,
the captain doubling over in laughter and the crew
jeering, too.

"Heads up!" the brawny sailor yelled, and the
pickle crock sailed through the air and splashed
down nearby.

With air stoppered up inside it, the crock floated.
As Luke swam to it, Abby could see he was in a
dead-white heat, angrier than she'd ever seen him.
But he didn't waste his breath on complaining as

waves splashed around them. "Let's go," Abby gasped when he was back at her side.

Kicking while clinging to the cork ring, Abby felt she was barely moving toward the distant shore of Manele Bay. *We have so far to go!* she thought. *How could the captain do this to us? What if there are sharks?* As if in answer to her fear, turbulence swirled next to her in the shadowed sea.

A second later a sleek gray body shot past her, surfaced with a *whoosh,* and dove underwater again. Abby's heart almost stopped with fear. She was going to be pulled under by a man-eating shark. "Luke!" she screamed.

In an instant he was beside her, but the long gray creature returned. This time it came within inches of Abby's side and hit the cork life ring with startling force. The life ring surged forward with the impact, and Abby moved with it. Luke stroked toward it one-handed, then hung on so Abby wouldn't lose it. *Whoosh!* Another breath exploded ahead of them, and this time Abby could see it clearly.

"It's a dolphin!"

"I'll be switched!" Luke exclaimed, trying to keep water from going down his windpipe. "There's a bunch of 'em."

Even from her low vantage point on the water, Abby could see puffs of water vapor, the dolphins' expelled breaths. Sure enough, they were in the middle of a dolphin school, and the creatures seemed curious about them.

One after another darted past them, often pushing against the life ring and sending them jetting forward several feet. Abby reached out a hand as one, breaking the surface with its dorsal fin, came toward her. When it swished by, her hand slid along its silky body—its skin as slippery smooth as a peeled, hard-boiled egg.

Fifteen minutes of kicking with occasional pushes by the dolphins brought them within reach of the white sand. Feeling the bay bottom beneath her feet, Abby fought against the tide to clamber ashore.

She and Luke collapsed on the sand. Abby fanned out her dress to dry in the breeze and took off her waterlogged boots. Her toes wiggled in the soft sand.

"Thunderation!" Luke said with enthusiasm. "That was a hoot!"

As the two caught their breath and rested, the shadows lengthened. Abby dug into their satchel. Their extra clothes were damp, so she laid them out to dry. "The map!" she said, extracting her sketchbook with a look of horror on her face. "It's wet."

She carefully unfolded it and lay it, too, on the sand to dry. "Oh, no, some of the ink has run. Luke, do you remember what was written here?"

Luke peered at it thoughtfully. "I didn't commit it to memory. Let's hope it wasn't important."

Abby pressed a hand to her forehead. Her temples were beginning to pound. "Must be around dinnertime." She wondered if Ma and Pa were sitting down with Uncle Samuel and little Sarah right now. Maybe they were heaping hot beans and cornbread on their plates, then bowing their heads to pray for Abby and Luke's safe return. *I hope Pa's not too mad. I hope they know we did it to help out the family. . . .*

She looked around the deserted beach, then turned to view the dry scrub brush and desolate hills behind the bay. Despair and loneliness engulfed her.

We're so alone! This isn't Maui, where friendly Hawaiians live. This is "spit-dry" Lanai.

Unbidden, Abby recalled Uncle Samuel's words: "*Lanai* means 'day of conquest.'" His words conjured up visions of people running in fear from violent warriors. As the breeze kicked up, Abby shuddered. She thought about the innocent families murdered here. *Could the island really be haunted?* A prickling sensation crawled across the back of her neck.

"Luke, do you . . . do you think it's safe to be here?" she asked cautiously. She anchored a rock on the map so it wouldn't blow away.

"It's a little late to worry about that now, Abby. Are you thinking about the stories of Lanai being haunted?"

"It's just so . . . deserted. And I have this feeling we're being watched." She peeked over her shoulder again at the landscape.

"There's no such thing as ghosts, Abby," he said firmly. Then, as if sensing her dark mood, he said lightly, "Besides, I've brought my lucky rabbit's foot—sure to keep bad spirits away." He winked at her, his green eyes darkening with the fading light.

She shivered again, but this time it was not from the cool ocean breeze. "Oh, *why* did we come?"

Luke put his hand on her shoulder. "We've just had a setback with that mean old Captain Jim," he said with a soothing tone. "But our treasure hunt *is* a good idea, Ab. . . . We're doing it to help your family, and that can't be bad." He gave her shoulder a squeeze of encouragement. "Hey, how about a drink of water?" He got up and walked to the crock and knelt down. Digging his knife into the top of the cork, he unplugged it and carried it back to her.

"Here, you get the first sip of fresh water," he offered.

Abby couldn't return his smile. Night was coming on fast, and they had no fire, no supper, and no blankets. Hungry and thirsty, she raised the heavy crock with both hands and put it to her lips.

One deep sip and Abby almost dropped the bottle in her haste to get it away from her lips. She choked, coughed, and sputtered. "Ahhh!"

"Abby? What's wrong?" Luke asked with concern.

"It's pickle juice!"

Luke threw back his head in a laugh. Abby watched him for a moment, then climbed to her feet with the jug in hand. "Luke, you're one rotten friend," she said out loud, but her eyes were shining with glee. Then she dumped the green juice over his head.

Luke leapt up as quick as a burnt frog. "Yuck!" he said as the juice drained down his face and into his open mouth.

Abby doubled over with merriment, falling down on the sand. Luke dropped back down on his knees with her. The sound of their joy temporarily drowned out the boom of the crashing waves.

"Race you to the water," Luke said as he bounced up again and ran toward the waves to wash pickle juice from his hair. Abby followed and dipped her toes in the frothy white seafoam.

As Luke dunked his head in the incoming wave, Abby spotted an astonishing sight in the bay. Dolphins were shooting out of the water in wild twisting leaps, splashing back down amid geysers of seawater. "Luke!" She waded out to him and touched his shoulder. "Look!"

They stood in the warm salt water, watching the sleek spotted dolphins spin from the water into the twilight. "Dozens of 'em putting on a show," Luke said in awe.

"It sounds like they're laughing, just like us," Abby said. The two stood, fascinated, until the animals headed out to deep water.

Then Luke looked heavenward. "The first star," he said, pointing. "I like this time of night—when the sky is turning sapphire blue."

"It's beautiful," Abby said, hope returning to her voice for the first time since coming ashore. "Let's

go start a fire and eat. Then we can make plans for
tomorrow's treasure hunt."

Together they gathered driftwood and set it
ablaze with Abby's watertight tin box of matches.
Luke headed toward a stream to wash out and refill
the pickle crock with fresh water.

When he returned, they munched soggy, salty
biscuits. They dreamed of the sparkling diamonds,
rubies, and gold they were bound to find the next
day.

"Maybe there will be so much jewelry," Abby
said, "that Ma will be able to keep some pieces for
herself."

"And your uncle will have more than enough
money to pay the king for his land. We'll restock
the ranch, too, and I can become a Hawaiian caball-
ero—a cowboy," Luke said, lazily gazing into the
flames. "Then I can make my own way in the world,
and I'll never have to go back to my aunt's house
again."

Abby thought about his mean aunt, Dagmar
Gronen, with whom he'd been forced to live when
his parents died. There was no one colder and more
controlling than that steely eyed woman. Sure, she
was rich, Abby thought, and that gave her a lot of
power. She always got her way! But she wasn't that
smart. . . . All her money hadn't gotten her what
Abby valued most: Luke's love and friendship.

When he'd arrived as an eleven-year-old orphan
from Pennsylvania, Abby had brought him home to

meet her family. Now at fourteen, Luke was part of the family, and she'd do anything to keep it that way. Her parents loved him as they did Abby and Sarah. And if Abby and Luke could find the treasure, they'd be rich, too. Everything was bound to work out.

Abby mounded sand for a pillow and put on her spare shirt and skirt to keep warm through the cool night breezes. She laid her head on the almost-empty satchel, facing the fire. Luke lay down on the other side of the fire pit and closed his eyes. The waves crashing on shore and the brilliance of the stars overhead made roughing it almost worthwhile, Abby thought. "It's peaceful and pretty, isn't it, Luke?" she asked.

"Mm-hmm," Luke drawled, almost asleep.

Abby closed her eyes and breathed in the fragrance of burning wood. Then a strange briny odor wafted over her. "Horse feathers!" Abby sat up and searched the area. "Is there rotting seaweed near us? What's that smell?"

Luke opened one eye and grinned. "Pickle juice."

Chapter Six

When Abby woke in the bright light, Luke was gone!

The sun had only recently risen, but she could already feel its heat. She stood, shading her eyes, and then she saw him. Shirt off and pants rolled up, he dove over and over into the ceaseless waves. As the sunlight danced through the blue-green water, Luke's tall body was outlined against the arcing surge.

"Luke!" she hollered, strolling toward him. To her delight, the dolphins were back. They circled the bay slowly, as if tired from a night of activity—fishing, she figured.

"*Aloha*, Abby!" Luke called as he emerged dripping from the sea. "I'm raring to go treasure hunting. Let's get out the map and plan our attack." He shook his head like a dog shakes off after a swim.

The two made their way back to the campsite and shared the one remaining biscuit. "If I don't get real food soon," Luke said, "I'm going to ask our friends to bring me a fish." He gestured toward the dolphins.

Abby agreed with him as she opened the map and smoothed it out on the sand. "I think this is Manele Bay," she said, pointing to the map, "where we are. If that's true, then we're east of the treasure and need to head west."

"Looks like we need to follow the coastline a few miles until we get here," Luke said, tapping the *X* on the map. He ran his fingers through his almost-dried hair. "Abby, I can't believe we didn't think about bringing a shovel! We'll probably have to dig up the treasure. How are we going to do that?" he exclaimed, looking stricken.

"It'll work out," she said, thinking back to how God had helped them escape Jackal and the *Flying Lady* months earlier. "First, we've got to find the treasure—before Jackal does. *That's* the thing to worry about." *Dear God, help us! I want to see Pa's eyes light up when Luke and I return with the gold!*

Abby stashed the map carefully between the pages of her journal and set it in the satchel. Luke took a last swig of water from the pickle jar, then got out his pocketknife and cut the rope off the life ring. "This'll help us carry the jug," he said, coiling the rope and tying it through the handle of the jar. He slung the rope and attached jug over one shoulder as Abby finished tying her bootlaces.

"Let's keep the ocean in sight," Luke said, "so we don't get lost inland."

An hour later, Abby was dusty, hot, and tired clear through. Her legs were beginning to feel numb around the ankles. "Luke, this island is bigger than I thought!"

"Let's head into that kukui grove," Luke said, pointing to the rising land to the north. "We can stay shaded in the forest, but we'll travel along the edge of it so we don't lose our bearings."

As they made their way under the trees' dappled shade, Abby sighed with relief. A soft breeze rustled the leaves overhead, and birds with brown and yellow feathers flitted from branch to branch. Far off in the distance, an unusual bird call echoed over and over. *E-o, e-o*, it repeated.

"Sounds sad, doesn't it?" Abby asked.

"Like we're all alone in the world," Luke answered. "Want to rest?"

Abby nodded, grateful he remembered how hard hiking was for her. They sat down on a log and sipped water. Sunlight filtered through breaks in the trees, and boulders dotted the landscape. Abby's eyes roved ahead and stopped on a pile of rocks; for a moment, her gaze was riveted. Then she walked toward the stones.

"Luke," she hollered in amazement, "come here and see this."

She bent down in the dust near the boulder, her

hand tracing the rock's smooth red face and the lines etched into it.

Luke came over and stopped short at what he saw. "Drawings?"

"They're called *petroglyphs*," Abby said. "I know because Uncle Samuel wrote to us about them once. He said they're from ancient times." The two stared at the stick figures on the rock's face, wondering who those long-ago people were. *E-o, e-o* came the distant cry again. The sun slipped behind a bank of clouds, casting them in shadows.

The sudden sense that something wasn't right flashed through Abby. She glanced up to see a shadow slip through the trees ahead of them. Whoever—or whatever—it was now crouched behind a boulder twenty feet away.

Abby's heart leapt into her throat. She remembered Uncle Samuel's and Captain Jim's words: "Some say the island is haunted."

"Luke," she whispered, keeping her eyes on the spot, "we're not alone!"

Luke scowled. "I know that, Abby. You've told me before, God is always with us." He shook his head as if she'd been out in the sun too long.

"No! Someone's behind that boulder up ahead."

Luke smiled at her, then turned to look in the direction she was staring. "And I suppose you're gonna tell me he's wearing an eye patch?"

Before Abby could reply, a figure darted out from

behind the rock and sprinted to a nearby thicket of kukui trees.

"I'll never doubt you again," Luke said in awe, easing the jug and rope down to the ground. "It looks too small to be a man."

"Unless it's . . ." Abby hardly dared voice her fears. "One of those spirits of the murdered innocents."

"Abigail, there's no such thing," Luke countered matter-of-factly. "Besides, he looks tanned; spirits are pale and white, aren't they?"

"I suppose you're right, but this means the island isn't deserted like Captain Jim said," Abby shot back. "What should we do?"

"Chase after him."

"But what if we don't catch him, or he can't speak English?" Abby countered. "Let's act like we don't see him; then he'll relax and get closer. Maybe we can become friends."

"That's a good idea," Luke said, opening the satchel and retrieving his second shirt. He wrapped the hemp rope in it. "I need padding. This is rubbing me raw," he explained. "All right, let's move on and keep an eye on him. I hope we meet up soon—I need food, and he probably knows where to get some—"

"On this spit-dry island," Abby said, finishing his thought. As she picked up their satchel, she hoped the stranger *would* prove friendly. But what if he wasn't? And why was he following them?

Chapter Seven

E-o, e-o. The haunting cries of the bird echoed
around them as Abby and Luke walked along the
edge of the forest. They were ever aware of the
person keeping even with them, only twenty or
thirty feet away, even though he ran quietly from
tree to tree. Luke decided Abby was right: They
should try to befriend him. So he began to sing an
old sea chanty he'd learned from Captain Chandler,
hoping it would make them sound friendly and
lighthearted. He shifted the jug and began:

> *Well, I miss my girlie from Californie*
> *Where the maidens all dance a jig;*
> *But the sea is fine and she's calling me;*
> *So I'll sleep here with my pig!*
> *Souu-eee!*

Abby giggled and Luke grinned over at her.
Suddenly, from behind a boulder to their right,
there was a snort that sounded like a stifled laugh.

"Shall I sing the next verse?" Luke asked Abby.
"Yes, please!"
"Here goes, then," Luke said, plunging in.

Though I love the ocean, this bunk seems small
With a pig whose tail's too curly,
So I'm leaving ye boys, to answer the call
And go marry my California girlie!
Hooo-eee!

Abby threw Luke a radiant smile when a definite laugh came from behind a rock eight feet ahead. "Well, you must speak English," Luke said playfully. "Why don't you come out and join us?"

The forest seemed to pause, as if it were holding its breath. Then a hand showed on top of the boulder and a head, framed in black cropped hair, popped up. When the boy stood up and came around the boulder, Luke saw he was thinner and younger than they were. Luke guessed the boy was probably about ten years old. He wore a *malo*, a loincloth, the typical Hawaiian dress for men until the missionaries arrived in 1820. His short hair shone like the blue-black wing of a raven, and his hesitant smile showed white teeth framed by a round, tanned face. He nervously fingered a leather thong around his neck that sported sharks' teeth.

Abby took a step toward him. "I'm Abby, and this is Luke," she said in a friendly tone.

He nodded once. "You song funny."

Luke smiled lazily, hoping he wouldn't spook him. "You want to learn it?" he asked.

The boy nodded again and eagerly came closer, seating himself on a rock across from Luke. As Luke sang it out once more, the boy grinned. When Luke finished, the stranger introduced himself. "I be Kini," he said, pointing at his chest, "son of Kono, grandson of Mako."

His English wasn't great, Luke thought, but good enough to share information—and hopefully news of food. "Glad to meet you, Kini. Is your family nearby?"

Kini's dark brown eyes grew serious, and he began to toy with his shark necklace. "Yes, family *mauka*—up mountain," he said, inclining his head toward the higher regions.

It was clear to Luke that Kini wasn't comfortable talking about his family. *Time to try another subject,* he thought. "Kini, do you know of any banana or mango groves around here? I'm as hungry as a bear after winter." As if to prove it, Luke's stomach grumbled loudly. Kini's smile returned as he heard it.

"Your stomach talk loud. Follow Kini. I take you to plenty papaya." Without a further word, he started off. The kids lost no time in picking up their gear and hurrying after him.

They headed inland, away from their view of the sea. Within minutes Kini had led them to a grove of papaya trees, heavily laden with large yellow fruit. Luke's eyes bugged at the sight. Abby reached up and plucked one that had a pink cast to it, and Luke opened his pocketknife.

The two sat down in grass under one of the trees as Kini inspected the ripe fruit and plucked off the best. He brought four more over, balancing them in his thin arms, and set them in Abby's lap. Then he sat beside her.

Luke sliced open the first one and dug out the round, black seeds. Then he and Abby dove into the sweet meat of the papaya like starving wolves, the red fruit smearing on their chins.

Kini looked on curiously. "Good?"

"Mm-hmm," Abby responded, "so sweet!"

Luke only grunted. Kini picked up the pocket-knife and smiled. "Knife good!"

Luke watched Kini cut into the next papaya and flick out the seeds. Then he handed each of them a half. Luke dove in again, but Abby ate more slowly now. He heard her make conversation as he finished and picked up another half Kini had prepared.

"My family lives on Oahu now," Abby explained. "We didn't know anyone lived on Lanai. Has your family been here long?"

Kini licked his lips. "Grandfather Mako bring us four years ago. We make village life like old fathers before us, before *haoles* come. Mako is *kahuna nui*. . . ." At this Kini again fingered his shark-tooth necklace and cleared his throat. It seemed to Luke that the boy actually shrunk in size as his shoulders hunched over. "Mako bring old gods to us. You know?"

Luke, completely confused by Kini's language, was silent. But Abby was nodding as if it all made sense. "I understand," she said. "Your grandfather is a priest, and he brought you and your family here to live the old way—to worship the old gods?"

Kini nodded vigorously. "Yes! The gods Queen Regent throw in sea. That make Mako mad like wild boar." He scowled and put a finger on either side of his mouth, imitating a wild boar with tusks. "Before that, Mother say Grandfather be kind. But he changed now, with anger always in his heart. He not . . . the same."

Abby inclined her head toward him. "So your mother and father are here, too?"

Kini had grown solemn. "Yes, and sister, Niha. She be a fly—always buzz near me, bother me."

Abby laughed out loud. "I have a little sister, too. And I know just what you mean . . . they can be pests!"

"She follow Kini too much," Kini said emphatically. "I hide."

Luke licked the sweet juice from his fingers and chin. "Abby's little sister, she's just like that!" But secretly he loved having Sarah around because he loved feeling like part of a family. His worst fear was that Abby's parents would make him return to California. But if he and Abby returned with gold, they were bound to see how valuable he could be.

Kini bent over Luke's pocketknife, opening and closing the blade in fascination. "Knife good," he murmured, holding it out to Luke with a trace of regret.

"Thanks," Luke said, taking it. He cleaned and dried the blade on his pants, reclosed the blade, then tossed it into the open satchel. He wished he could give it to Kini, but they'd need it before the treasure hunt was over.

"Luke," Kini asked, "what's this 'bear' you say about?"

"A bear? You don't have bears here?"

Kini shook his head no.

"Bears are big," Luke explained, as he stood up with his arms stretched over his head. "Grizzlies are the meanest. They could kill a man with the swipe of a paw." He pantomimed a bear swiping this way and that as Kini's eyes got big.

Abby saw Kini's face. "What do you have here in Hawaii to be afraid of?"

"*Mako,*" Kini answered quickly. "As *haole* say, shark."

Luke stopped bear-acting. "Isn't Mako the name of your grandpa?"

Kini looked away. "Yes."

Abby and Luke exchanged glances of alarm. "Sounds like your grandpa is pretty tough," Luke said.

Kini cracked his finger joints. "Shark be the god of my grandfather. He hate *haole* god. Priests of the white man's god, they make change in land. Grandfather say not good."

"Do you mean the missionaries, Kini? Is your grandfather mad at the missionaries who've brought changes?" Abby asked, incredulous.

Kini agreed. "Yes! Miss . . . on . . . aries."

"My uncle told me that Kaahumanu, Queen Regent, threw the Hawaiian idols into the sea *before* the missionaries came," Abby anxiously began.

Luke spoke up. "And I thought the missionaries taught the people how to read, which is good. Hey, didn't the islanders used to sacrifice people to idols?"

At Luke's words, Kini jumped up, announcing abruptly, "I go now." With that he ran off up the hill, weaving through the bright green trees of the surrounding kukui forest.

"Luke, you asked too many questions!" Abby crossed her arms in irritation.

Luke looked chagrined as they watched Kini disappear through the kukui grove. "I guess I did. Didn't mean to scare him off. . . . Maybe we should go after him and apologize?"

"That's a good idea," Abby said shortly. "Let's go." She bent over to retrieve their satchel.

Luke grabbed two more papayas. "For dinner," he said, stashing them in the satchel and carrying it for Abby.

They pushed up the hill, following Kini's trail. Although they hollered a few times, Kini was either too far ahead to hear them or didn't want to answer.

After fifteen minutes of scrambling over logs, around trees, and through brush, Abby flopped down on a boulder. "Luke, I've got to rest. Maybe we just need to let Kini go."

Luke could see she was breathing hard. "Yeah, let's make camp here. This crock is heavier than a bushel of apples, and I'm hungry again." With that he began gathering dried limbs and brush. He dropped his first load near her and headed off to collect more.

Abby collected rocks to form a campfire ring.

When Luke returned with more wood, he knelt to help Abby form the fire pit. "Hey, you want to try broiled papaya for dinner?" he asked hopefully.

She laughed. "Guess it's the only thing on the menu, huh?"

He tweaked her nose. "That's the spirit. Tomorrow's bound to be the day we find gold."

"It will be," she said confidently. Then she handed him the matches and opened her journal, beginning to record with her pencil all that had happened since they boarded the *Beauty* in Lahaina. When Luke blew on the fire, she asked, "I wonder why Kini seemed upset when you asked about his grandfather?"

Luke answered without glancing up from his task. "I get the feeling he's afraid."

"Afraid of what?"

"I dunno." He paused. "His grandpa, I guess. Didn't he say they're living the old way?"

Abby chewed the end of her pencil. "Yes. But why would that make him afraid of his grandpa?"

Luke grunted between blowing puffs of air on the fire. "Maybe 'cause he's powerful? You know more about this stuff than me."

"Hmm . . . it's true the priests—the *kahunas*—had a lot of power. They were in charge of all the rules the common people had to obey. Uncle Samuel said it was a system of *kapu*. *Kapu* is something that's taboo, or off limits. If someone—even a child—broke a *kapu*, he was punished severely. I think he could even be killed, but that seems hard to believe. The Hawaiians we've met have been so loving, so filled with *aloha*. And Uncle Samuel told me a foreigner had never been killed . . . so they must not apply the same rules to us." Abby thought of Olani, her kind and gracious friend. "All that must have happened a long, long time ago."

The fire roared into a blaze and Luke moved back. "But something doesn't feel right with Kini."

As soon as Luke said the words, Abby shivered. Both of them knew he'd spoken the truth. As the forest's gloom darkened and shadows lengthened, how glad she was that the fire burned brightly!

She returned to her journal and wrote, "Wish I knew the secret Kini didn't want to share . . . or is afraid to share."

Chapter Eight

That night, Abby admired the stars through a canopy of swaying trees. She and Luke talked about the treasure again as they watched the flames consume the logs.

"Maybe I'll melt down some doubloons to make gold cowboy spurs," he said.

Abby chuckled. "You're shameless."

We've just got to find those riches, Abby thought as she rose to prepare for bed. She swished her mouth out with pickle-smelling water and thought of her ma and pa, how one of them always came to her bed and prayed over her. She missed them.

The cool night wind picked up, turning the overhead trees into dancing shapes that sometimes blotted out the starlight. A haunting loneliness swept through Abby even though Luke was just across the fire pit from her.

She folded her second skirt into a pillow and draped her other shirt about her shoulders like a short blanket. When she heard Luke snoring, she lay down and prayed for a safe sleep. But sleep wouldn't come. Each time she began to doze, a strange noise would startle her, waking her fully. Twice she felt as if something had brushed against her hair. Was it only the wind?

Uneasy, she sat up and looked at Luke across the fire pit. The flames had burned low and turned into red and gray embers. Luke's mouth hung open and a light snore issued forth. *This is silly*, she thought. *We're just camping outdoors. There are no wild animals to attack us. We're safe.* But the fear remained, making her heart beat hard against her rib cage.

Abby couldn't shake the feeling that something was amiss. *God is always with me. He's always with me . . .* , she kept telling herself.

She lay back down. Holding perfectly still for over an hour to listen for any unusual noise, Abby never noticed when she finally fell to sleep.

It was the same nightmare. She hung along the side of a ship, the deep sea below her. Jackal leered down at her as she clung to a rope ladder that bounced against the ship's side. She watched in horror as the pirate put one hand on the hilt of his twelve-inch dagger. His hands weren't bound! He was free to come after her.

She was caught! If she climbed up, he'd grab her. If she fell into the deep blue sea, a shark could get her. Her heart started to pound. Seeing no way out, she began to scream.

Then, suddenly, someone was shaking her, so she screamed again. Her eyes flew open. Although she could barely see him since the night was black and the fire was almost out, she knew it was Luke. He was kneeling above her, one hand gripping her shoulder.

"Abby, you're having a nightmare," Luke said, sounding concerned.

She swallowed hard and shook her head to clear the terror. "Luke, it was horrible! I was trapped, and I didn't know what to do." She couldn't stop trembling.

In the moment before Luke spoke again, Abby heard a thrumming sound. Her eyes went wild. "Something's after us!" She leapt up and searched the area desperately.

"No, Abby. You're hearing drums. It's been going on for a while." Luke rose and patted her back. "I think it must be coming from Kini's village up ahead. It woke me before you screamed. You're okay now. You're safe."

"It . . . it was just a bad dream, I guess," she said, feeling foolish. But the drums kept beating. She reached instinctively for her little gold cross hanging around her neck, Luke's birthday present to her last year.

"Why don't we head over that rise and see if we can spy on Kini's village?" he suggested. "I wonder what they're doing. I'd like to see how the natives lived before the white man came, wouldn't you?"

"No!" Her eyes dilated. "No, I . . . I don't think that's a good idea. I think we should stay by the fire and wait for morning . . . don't you?"

"Naw, I'm wide awake anyhow. Let's go spy on 'em! Come on, an opportunity like this doesn't come along every day."

"Luke, I don't want to go."

"All right, you sit tight, and I'll be back in an hour or so." He bent over, grabbed the water jug and took a sip, then replugged it.

Panicked, Abby looked around the campsite. The firelight was almost gone; the wind made eerie noises as it blew the trees above her. She couldn't sit there alone! "I'm going with you."

"Great," he said as he started up the incline toward the drums. Abby hurried after him, checking fearfully over her shoulder. But then she had the distinct impression that the danger was not behind them, but *ahead* of them—lying in wait.

They hiked slowly in the dark to avoid swaying tree limbs and roots. After twenty minutes of climbing

uphill, they began a gentle descent. From this
vantage point they could see fires glowing red-
orange in the valley spread below them. They made
their way quietly down the incline toward the light
and pounding drums. When Luke stopped
abruptly, Abby ran into his back.

He motioned for her to hide behind a boulder as
they took in the scene. A village of grass huts
covered a few acres of land in the valley; the perime-
ter was ringed by trees. Campfires burned in front
of several of the huts. But the largest fire burned in
the center of the village, and a large group of people
had gathered there.

Native men beat gourd drums, the kind Abby
had seen Olani use. Ten dressed in traditional *malos*
with garlands of coconut leaves around their wrists
and ankles danced before the fire in wild motions.
As Abby and Luke watched, the male dancers
picked up torches and began twirling them around
and around in the darkness. They skillfully threw
them high into the air and caught them as they
crashed back to earth in an arc of golden light.

Luke drew in his breath. "They're *good*."

Abby watched silently. The beat picked up speed
for several minutes, and the rotations of firebrands
flew more quickly through the air, spinning circles
of dizzying light. As the drums drove on to a rising
crescendo, the firebrands arced higher and landed
in the dancers' outstretched hands with a flourish.
At the same moment the drumbeats roared, then

suddenly quit, and the dancers threw themselves flat on the ground, their torches flung before them.

A collective gasp went up from the crowd. They kneeled in homage as a man dressed in a flowing red-and-yellow cape and matching helmet stood up. He spoke words Abby and Luke couldn't understand. From inside the largest hut emerged another man, old and shriveled, but also dressed in cape and helmet. In his gnarled hands he bore the feathered image of a snarling face, its gaping mouth permanently fixed open.

As the old priest walked forward, all the people sank to the ground, lying facedown. He set the idol on a large pile of stones, removed his helmet, and bowed down to the ground before it. *The whole village is bowing down to this idol!* Abby thought, scared. What would they do if they discovered her and Luke?

She jumped when Luke touched her hand. "Your hands are cold. I think it's time to go. This . . . this isn't what I expected," he said, sounding shaky.

She took one last glimpse of the valley before her. "Let's get out of here."

As they headed back down the hill and toward their campsite, she was glad Luke didn't let go of her hand. He gripped it firmly while Abby's thoughts returned to the vision of the idol, which strangely reminded Abby of something . . . of someone.

"Jackal!" she cried.

"Where?" Luke said, his eyes darting about as he pulled her toward a tree trunk. He intended to hide, but Abby shook her head and stopped walking.

"Not here," she said, almost breathless. "It was the idol—its teeth remind me of him. What if he's here—on the island?"

Even in the dark she could see Luke's face harden as he spoke. "Then we better hurry up and get that gold."

The morning sun had not yet dawned, but the sky had turned pale gray when Abby first opened her eyes. Her night terrors were gone, and her stomach was growling. When she heard movement behind her, Abby sat up. "Luke?"

He was roaming around the campsite. "Where's the satchel, Abby? I need my knife to chop open this papaya."

She rubbed her eyes and yawned. "Didn't you use it to sleep on?"

"No, I thought you did."

"Hmm." Abby got up and shook out her wadded-up skirt, then realized there was no satchel in which to put it. "It has to be here." She turned in all directions around their campsite. That's when she saw the figure farther up the hill.

"Luke!" She pointed to the small figure with long black hair that was darting through the trees and shrubs up the hill.

"Come on!" Luke took off like greased lightning while Abby was still tying the laces on her ankle-high boots.

She grabbed her shirt, skirt, and the rope-bound pickle crock and took off after Luke. Though he was already far ahead of her, she could easily spot him and follow. But within minutes she was wishing he'd picked up the water crock.

Fifteen minutes later, Abby realized they were moving toward Kini's village, and she'd lost sight of Luke. For a split second, her heart pounded with the fear that he'd left her alone, until she almost ran smack-dab into him. "Ugh, Luke!" He'd popped up from behind a fern and pulled her instantly down to a crouch.

"Shh," he warned with a finger to his lips. Confused, Abby didn't understand until he peered over the large boulder in front of them and pointed. There, beyond them, lay the valley they'd seen the night before. A few fires burned low in pits, but what interested Abby most was the sight of Kini carrying their satchel into the still-sleeping village. Trailing far behind him was a little girl with long, swaying hair, who had to be about six years old. Abby guessed it was Niha, Kini's sister. It was obvious he didn't know she was following him. *But it was a good thing she had,* Abby thought, *or we wouldn't have known Kini took our satchel!*

Kini disappeared behind a hut at the distant edge of the village. Luke sank back down. "That pint-sized rascal stole our stuff!" Luke whispered, his voice angry.

"How are we going to get back our map?"

"My knife," Luke muttered, tossing a stick angrily.

Abby heaved a sigh. "I know it's important, but it's not as valuable as the treasure map!"

"Naw, I mean he was after my knife. The little thief! When I get my hands on him . . ."

Abby thought for a moment. "I don't see why we can't just go get it. Everything I've learned about Hawaiians has shown me they're kind and generous. If we go in and ask politely, I know Kini will give it back. And I doubt he'll even know what the map is for."

Luke looked skeptical. "You think they're gonna hand it back, after stealing it? Do you remember the scene we witnessed last night?"

"Yes, but he's just a big-eyed kid—and might even get a whipping for it. I know they're living the old way, but Hawaiians have always been kind to outsiders. It's the *aloha* way."

Luke frowned, then sighed. "All right. As soon as the village rises, I'm game. We just walk right in?"

Abby paused, remembering the night scene they'd witnessed. But the dawning sun made her nighttime fears recede. "Yes, we walk right in," she said confidently. "Have a little faith in God, you rascal," she said as she handed him the heavy crock to carry.

The village soon came to life as the sun's rays beat down on the fronds of the thatched huts. Fires were stoked, and children ran along the dirt pathways. The scent of baking fish and breadfruit rose on the slight breeze. "It's time," Abby said. "Come on. I'm sure they'll have your favorite—*poi!*" She'd never forget Luke's wry face as he tried the mushy purple mixture that the islanders loved.

"If they serve us *poi,* I'll know they're out to get us," Luke grumbled as she dragged him from behind the boulder and through the trees at the edge of the clearing.

They had only taken a few steps into the clearing when a dog howled and raced toward them, its fangs bared. Several men looked up from their conversation and stalked toward the newcomers. Their eyes were suspicious—as if they hadn't seen *haoles* once they'd settled on Lanai.

Abby stood rooted to the ground. Her heart pounded as she saw their fierce expressions, but she smiled broadly. "*Aloha!*"

They stopped and mumbled among themselves. "*Aloha, haole* girl." The tall man who spoke was fierce-looking, with long curly hair and untrusting eyes. He had a white scar that ran down his cheek and, as all the men, wore the traditional *malo*. "How you come to Lanai?"

This was not the kind of greeting Abby had imagined, but she tried her best to be friendly. "We've come from Maui on an errand for my parents. Yesterday we met Kini down the hill," she said, pointing in the general direction from which they'd come. "We came to speak with him about our . . . something." She instantly realized she didn't want to get Kini in trouble. Maybe he'd give back the satchel and she wouldn't have to tell anyone. Besides, the less people who knew about the map, the better.

"Kini!" one of the men yelled. The shout was taken up by several others until Kini's head peered out of his hut, and he came scampering through the village toward the men.

When he neared them, his eyes almost popped out of their sockets. Abby saw fear flit across his face as he slowed to a walk and approached them. His thin shoulders caved in, and he licked his lips. Niha came running behind him as fast as her little legs could carry her. *Just like Sarah,* she thought, and she was glad she hadn't told on Kini.

Scar Cheek, who had first spoken to her, eyed her seriously. "What you need to speak of him for?"

Abby saw a tremor pass through Kini. *Why is he so afraid?* "We want to thank you, Kini, for helping us find papaya yesterday. We were very hungry."

Kini's uncertainty gave way to a slight smile. A woman with a round, kind face walked toward him and put her hand possessively on his shoulder. "You are welcome here. Come, *kamali'i*, eat *pu-pus*."

By the way she touched Kini, Abby was sure this was his mother. "Thank you so much! We are very hungry this morning, too." The sweet-faced woman smiled at her. She wore a wraparound dress, and her dark hair was piled on her head with a tortoise comb. Her kind spirit immediately reminded Abby of Olani, and she felt at ease. Abby nudged Luke as if saying, "I told you so." But when she did, Scar Cheek scowled at her.

As they followed Kini and his mother toward their hut, a few nodded to them, but only one smiled. Most looked concerned, as if the presence of strangers might be trouble. *This is so different from other Hawaiian villages,* Abby thought. *These people are shy!* When they arrived at Kini's hut, the woman introduced herself as Malie, Kini's mother. She insisted they sit on rough *tapa* mats in front of the hut and rest while she began to prepare breakfast. Kini sat with them, but Abby didn't want to discuss their satchel yet. She and Luke were riveted by a scene taking place just yards away.

A teenage boy stood beside a pile of coconuts, apparently collected from a recent beach foray. As Abby watched, he picked up a thick-husked nut and rammed it down on a pointed shaft of wood stuck in the ground. His bronzed arm muscles flexed in the sunlight. With blinding speed he ripped the thick wooden husk from the huge nut and discarded it. Then he flipped the coconut until he found a line running through it. He hit the shell hard on the spear point, and the coconut split into two clean halves, frothy milk spilling out into a bowl below him.

Abby suddenly remembered Uncle Samuel splitting the apple. "The Lord put special talents in each one of you," he'd said. *Oh, Lord, let one of my talents be finding the gold so we can help my parents and Uncle Samuel!* she prayed. *And let it be as easy for us as breaking coconuts is for this islander.*

Back on Oahu Abby had tried to smash a coconut with Pa's hammer, and the hammer had bounced off it. But this youth made it look simple! When he'd done about ten of them, he caught Abby watching. He smiled at her and brought the next split coconut over, carefully preserving the milk in one half. "Here, *nani wahine*," he said shyly. He held the coconut out to Abby; she took it and drank deeply.

"Mmm, it's good." She smiled back.

Luke took the coconut and took a sip. "What'd he say?"

Abby's face burned red. "He said, 'Here, pretty female.' "

Luke snorted as Malie came toward them bearing a tray of baked leaves. She motioned for Luke to open the leaves and taste whatever was inside. "Do you think it's *poi?*" Luke asked.

"No *poi,*" Malie answered. "Breadfruit and coconut. You like?"

Luke took a small bite. "Abby, it's good!" He dug in with enthusiasm.

Abby eagerly reached out her hand, but Malie pulled the tray away. Shocked that Malie had offered the breakfast tray to Kini instead of to her, Abby waited. Malie set the tray down before the boys and put her hand out to Abby.

She pulled Abby up and took her inside the hut, where she motioned her to sit. Abby used the moment to remove her bonnet and glance around for their satchel. She still hadn't caught sight of it when Malie returned, carrying another tray of steaming leaves. She offered them to Abby, who unwrapped one and bit into it.

"Delicious, sweet, and moist. Malie, thank you."

Malie motioned toward the tray, and Abby helped herself to more. Niha, Kini's younger sister, joined them. Abby was delighted to be part of their little gathering in the hut but wondered why she wasn't allowed to eat with the boys.

Malie reached over and took one of her own creations. Then, as if in answer to Abby's silent question, she spoke. "It be *kapu* to eat with *kanaka*—the men. *Wahine*—women—eat separate."

"*Kapu?* Oh, this is part of living the old way?"

"Yes, *kapu.* Some things, as you say, be . . . not

allowed. *Kapu* for men and women to eat together. *Kapu* for *wahine* to eat wild boar, shark, banana."

"Ahh," Abby said. Uncle Samuel had not told her about this *kapu*—that men and women couldn't eat together. But he'd been right about Hawaiians. They, like Malie and Olani, were gracious and giving.

But as she savored the sweet breadfruit, a question arose in the back of her mind. *What other* kapus *has Uncle Samuel forgotten to mention?*

Chapter Nine

After breakfast, Kini showed Luke and Abby around his village, explaining more about how his grandfather, the *kahuna nui* of the village, had brought them here to live the old lifestyle. "So our chants and hula never die," he said. Everything about it sounded good, except for the *kapus* and the idol worship, but Abby didn't mention that. For a while they watched women press sheets of *tapa* against wide flat stones. Made from the paper mulberry bush, *tapa* became cloth for *malos* and dresses.

They saw men working on taro roots, washed white like peeled potatoes. The men ground the pale roots against well-worn granite with grinding stones, mashing them to a thick paste. They rolled and kneaded the taro like bread dough. Abby stood entranced with the quick skill she witnessed. "When we let sit in bowl for a time, it become *poi*," Kini explained. *Ah*, thought Abby, *that explains why it tastes fermented.*

Finally, Luke asked with a hint of impatience, "Where is our satchel, Kini? We have to be going soon."

Kini looked around to make sure no one overheard. He bowed his head and scuffed the dirt with his bare toes. "I . . . I take . . . your knife-blade . . . it good, and . . . I wanted." His brown eyes were luminous and sincere. "I sorry, Abby, Luke."

"It's all right, kid." Luke rubbed his chin. "Just get it for us and we'll let bygones be bygones."

Kini pointed toward the trees. "We go get now. I put it in hiding place so no one sees. Not far."

As Kini led the way into the trees, Abby and Luke followed. The shadowed forest was cool. They hadn't walked long when Abby saw a stone wall in the distance. "What is that, Kini?"

Kini slowed his pace. His face somber, he whispered his answer. "That be city of refuge. It is place where people come to escape death."

Luke's face was etched with confusion. "Talk English, Kini. What do you mean?"

Kini slowly led the way toward the tall, red-rock enclosure. "When people break *kapu,* they can be killed dead. If they come here—go over wall to hide—they be safe. You understand? It be *city of refuge.*" He said it emphatically, willing them to grasp his meaning.

Abby took in the wide ring of rocks and the grass hut roof that showed above the wall. "No one is allowed to chase the *kapu*-breaker and kill him if he makes it to the city of refuge?" she asked.

Kini spoke solemnly. "Yes, it be so—long ago. But . . . not always now." They had arrived at the stone enclosure, and Kini touched the rock wall, which was about five feet high.

He took a deep breath and patted the wall. "This place no one come to except when break *kapu*. That why it be good place for hiding things. But Abby, you not see over wall. You too, Luke. No look inside."

Before Abby could ask him why, Kini had nimbly climbed over the stone wall and leapt down inside the enclosure. They could no longer see him but could hear him moving toward the grass hut in the center of the "city."

Abby tapped her toe for a minute, then hummed a tune. Curiosity finally got the best of her. "Luke, why shouldn't we look? A little peek can't hurt!" She stuck the toe of her boot into a rock crevice and began to pull herself up the wall. Halfway up, she found herself stuck.

"Want a leg up?" Luke teased. He cupped his hands and Abby stepped into them as he pushed her foot upward. She gripped the top of the rock wall, resting her stomach on it until she swung her legs over as she attempted to sit on the edge. But she lost her balance and pitched forward. Landing with a teeth-jarring thud on the grass within the walls, Abby crumpled to her hands and knees. She touched something half-hidden in the grass.

A bloodcurdling scream erupted from her lips. Shocked, Luke vaulted over the wall. There, next to Abby in the tall grass, were bleached bones!

Chapter Ten

"Don't look, Abby!" Luke jumped down and turned her face into his arms.

"Let's go," she urged. He boosted her up onto the top of the wall, then climbed over and reached up to help her down.

When she was safely on the other side, Abby's blue eyes pierced his. "I thought this was the *city of refuge!*"

At that moment, Kini leapt down from the wall with the satchel in hand. "I tell you—no look!"

"Kini, who killed that person?" Abby asked excitedly, her pulse speeding. "I thought you said a person was safe once they made it to this refuge!"

"As I say, it be that way long ago," Kini said anxiously. "But my grandfather be mad—too mad one day—and he chase someone inside walls of refuge. He do this! He break *kapu* by chasing . . . nice old man." Kini's shoulders shook with his heaving sobs. Luke looked on, mortified, but Abby's face softened. She reached out and put her arms around Kini, who buried his face in her shoulder and clung tightly.

Over his head, Luke and Abby's eyes met. "Oh Kini," she said kindly, "I'm so sorry." *Now we understand why you are afraid of Mako!*

After a few minutes, Kini pulled back and searched Abby's eyes. The pain he'd been hiding showed clearly. Though he was calming down, his breath came in gulps and his nose was running. Luke found an old handkerchief in his back pocket, but he had to show Kini what it was for. Kini blew hard into the hankie and whispered, "*Mahalo,*" as he handed the drenched kerchief back to Luke.

Seemingly oblivious to Luke's discomfort, Kini turned to Abby. "Why my grandfather break *kapu*? He chase Palu into city of refuge, where he safe . . . but he kill him here." He shook his head. "He not live by old ways when he do this! Mako break *kapu!* Old way is to have place where people always safe."

"Kini," she began, "thirty years ago your queen threw the old gods into the sea because they are made of wood and stone. Idols can't eat. They can't talk. They can't help you. Your queen became a Christian because she learned about the One True God. He is the only One who can help you—who can keep you safe. There's a book that tells all about Him—the Bible. It calls Him our Stronghold, our *place of refuge.*"

Abby reached out and took Kini's hand. "If you

break *kapu,* if you sin, you can run to Him. The One True God will forgive you and keep you safe."

Kini's dark eyes bored intently into hers. "You know this One True God?"

"Yes, I know Him. He has been my *city of refuge* for a long time."

As if he were satisfied with her answer, Kini nodded. "I want to learn more about this One True God. You will teach me, Abby?"

She smiled. "Yes, but let's not stay here. Is there someplace we can go to talk?"

"You like to swim?" Kini asked.

"Yep," Luke answered as he discreetly dropped the soggy handkerchief behind his back and kicked it under a log.

"Then we go to sacred pool. Plenty mango there, too, so Luke not be hungry like a big greasy bear." Kini grinned, proud that he had remembered the wild creature's name.

Luke snorted, but spoke kindly. "That's grizzly bear, Kini."

The sun grew hot and the winds died down as they followed Kini. *This will be a treat,* Abby thought. She was glad to be away from that horrible place. She was doubly glad Kini seemed happier.

"It be early," Kini explained as they walked, "before royal ones come to bathe."

As Abby entered the glade of the sacred pool, she could smell the difference immediately. The air was moist and fragrant with the pungent scent of ginger and plumeria. The deep green water glistened in the late afternoon sunlight, beckoning her to enter its cool refreshment.

When Luke saw the glade, he yelled with pleasure. "Tadpoles, here I come!"

Kini raced ahead barefoot and ran lightly over the rocks near the shore. He took a flying leap and made a clean shallow dive into the waters.

Luke ran after him, flinging his shirt off as he went. He had been barefoot for hours, so he too ran into the pool with a gigantic splash. When he came up for air, he was grinning from ear to ear. "Just like back home in Coyote Creek!"

Abby had to sit on a log to take off her boots. Then she waded out gingerly into the cool water. When Luke squirted her with a stream from his mouth, she jumped back. "What's wrong, Abby? Don't like water?"

Abby splashed him a good one, and he dove under and disappeared. In a moment she learned where he'd gone when her leg was yanked and she was dunked underwater. When she came up, hair dragging over her face, he laughed at her. She tried to chase him down, but she was too weighted with waterlogged clothes. Eventually, however, he let her catch him and dunk him once, just to be fair.

Kini's jet-black hair stuck to his head as he climbed out of the pool and leapt off a tall rock. When he surfaced, he shook off water droplets. "Deep water here," he said with a grin. "Safe to jump."

"I don't think so!" Abby shuddered at the thought of jumping from that height.

After a while, they sat in the sun to dry off. Abby grew tired, but Luke and Kini just grew hungry. "I go pound taro for my mother. You come soon to eat evening meal. You come soon," he repeated. "Royal ones be here later." With that he waved and walked back toward the village.

"I *am* getting a mite hungry," Luke said, rubbing his belly.

Abby was perched on a large hot boulder; she'd spread her skirt out in the sun to dry. The fresh water had felt good. Now she lay back to rest. "Tomorrow we really have to make up for this day we've taken off. We've got to get the gold and head back. And Luke . . ." She searched for the right words. "I'd rather take our leave tonight before they . . . bow down to idols again."

"Reckon you're right, Ab. Can you find your way back to the village?" Luke asked.

"Of course!"

"Then I'm off. You never know—Malie might want me to sample some of her cooking. Don't be too long."

She waved good-bye and closed her eyes, resting peacefully by the fragrant pool. It felt good to be clean. *It feels good to be alive. Soon we'll have the gold. But before we leave tonight, I have to tell Kini more about Jesus. Otherwise, he might never hear.*

Abby thought about all she'd seen and learned since coming to Lanai. *Sarah will be sorry she missed another adventure, but I'll share all the details with her. Now I'll just rest for a minute or two. . . .*

In the hot sun, Abby fell fast asleep.

A loud noise, like a trumpet, penetrated Abby's consciousness. By the time she sat up and rubbed her eyes, fierce-looking Scar Cheek was blowing a conch shell and striding toward her. The loud sound jolted Abby, and she jumped off the rock and stood at attention as a procession of six men came quickly toward her.

They were on their way to the sacred pool, she realized. The third man in the middle of the line was huge in girth and height. He wore the traditional *malo,* a long red-and-yellow feathered cape, and an ivory carving of a fishhook hung around his neck. As they marched toward the pool, Abby recognized him as the chief she'd seen the night before.

The man behind him also looked royal, for he wore a feathered helmet and carried a club, but she couldn't see his face. He stalked with his head down to the ground. They strode directly toward her, the fierce-looking Scar Cheek blowing the conch shell harder and louder with each step. Abby wanted to bolt from the spot but felt an unnamed dread. Scar Cheek was almost upon her, and she was afraid to move.

From the corner of her eye, she saw Luke streaking toward her. "Abby!" The frantic sound of his voice alerted her to danger, but too late she realized it had to do with the men who were now upon her.

The first two men were passing her, and the chief was almost beside her on his way to the sacred pool.

"Abby, get down!" Luke yelled, but she didn't understand what he meant. The large chief with the fishhook necklace had just passed by when the *kahuna* behind him raised his club and took aim—at her!

In that split second Abby's stunned mind told her to crouch. As she did, Luke sprinted the last few paces to her, intercepting the priest's upraised club. He grabbed it with both hands, channeling the *kahuna's* aim away from Abby's skull. As the enraged priest struggled against Luke, Abby caught a look at his face. It was Mako! Both Luke and Mako grunted with fierce effort, but the skirmish lasted only seconds before another native behind Mako came to his aid and grabbed Luke's arms. Bound from behind, Luke screamed, "Run, Abby!"

Obeying him blindly, she leapt up and ran. She didn't understand why, but the dark emotions swirling across Mako's face told her he was intent on murdering her!

Abby raced away from the pool toward the forest. Feet pounded behind her. *I need a hiding place!* But she never made it into the trees' cover, for strong hands gripped her a moment later, whipping her around to face Scar Cheek. His voice shook with rage. "You break *kapu!*"

"*No!*" Luke screamed, anguish contorting his face. Abby knew then that somehow he'd found out about another *kapu* and had tried to warn her. But what had she done to break their ancient rules?

Mako came up to Abby, slapping her across the face. "You steal *mana!*" He spat in contempt on the ground in front of her.

"I . . . I didn't mean to . . . " Abby said, bewildered. She searched his face and realized there would be no mercy for her. Kini's heart-wrenching sobs came back to her. "I'm sorry. What can I do?" she asked in a small voice.

The renegade priest laughed. "You pay. For breaking *kapu.*"

Luke's face paled and he gasped.

Abby stared helplessly into the unyielding eyes of Mako, whose god was a shark. Anger surged through her. "You're not even a true priest of Hawaii! You break *kapu,* too!"

She earned another slap for her honesty.

Chapter Eleven

Pushed roughly along the path back to the village, Abby couldn't believe she was living through such a nightmare. *What have I done that is so awful they're treating me this way?*

Luke was also being herded roughly along the path. When she tripped, he bent down beside her and helped her up. The three men guarding them yelled angrily and thrust them forward. "Abby," Luke said anyway, daring to risk it, "I hope you can fast-talk us out of this one."

Tears stung her eyes. She had never felt so hated before. How could she talk them out of this mess when she didn't even know what she'd done to get into it?

Soon they burst out of the shadowed canopy of trees to the open village. People stopped what they were doing to stare in awe. Then the awe turned to fear when they saw Mako's furious face, and many turned away.

A smoldering ember of dread began to burn low

in Abby's stomach. The oppression she'd felt the night before when the people had bowed down to their idol returned.

A path opened up before them as they proceeded toward two stakes that had been thrust in the ground. While most people drew away from them, Abby noticed thin Kini coming toward them, his face a mask of concern. His little sister, Niha, was trailing him as usual. Abby immediately thought of Sarah and wished she were back home. Fear surged through her. *I want to go home! But what if—what if I can never go home again?*

Abby was thrust onto her knees, then pushed into a sitting position. Scar Cheek bound a rope around her and the stake. Abby's arms were wrapped at her sides like a spider wraps its victim before it devours it. Fifty feet away Luke was bound to another stake.

Quiet stole over the area—the laughter of children, which had been so prevalent minutes before, was silenced. Most had been hurried off to their huts; the few who remained outdoors were clinging to their mothers' sides or staying on the fringe of the distant crowd. Kini stood closer than anyone, his dark eyes questioning. Suddenly he took a step backward, and Abby followed his fearful gaze.

Striding toward them was Kini's grandfather—Mako. From her position on the ground, he loomed even larger and more powerful. Abby's blood pulsed in her ears. The aged *kahuna* did not bother to look at her as he spoke to the others in their native language. The men bowed, then proceeded to answer him. What were they saying? She searched Luke's tormented face, hoping to find an answer.

Kini's intake of breath riveted Abby's attention. Malie stood at the edge of the crowd, holding Niha protectively against her leg. When Kini turned and fled, Niha burst into tears.

Mako glared down at Abby, the full intensity of his hatred clear. When he stalked away, Abby screamed, "Let us go! Why are you doing this to us?"

Then the people of the village evaporated like a mist at noon. Everyone went into their huts, leaving them completely alone.

Abby hung her head dejectedly. An hour or two had passed, but Abby had lost track of time. She was so distraught she couldn't think clearly.

The soft padding of little feet on dirt brought her head up. Niha was coming shyly toward her, carrying a gourd of water. Even from a distance Abby could see it was water, for the six year old was slopping it with every step.

As Niha neared, Abby looked into the sweet face with the dusky eyes and pink lips. A red sarong was wrapped about her, and a pink flower lei adorned her neck. Her long black hair flowed over her shoulders as she leaned down to offer Abby water from the gourd.

Abby took a few sips. "*Mahalo*, Niha," she said softly. "Thank you." When she took another sip, some of it spilled down her dress, and Niha giggled. It sounded loud in the deserted village.

"Do you know what they're going to do with us, Niha?" Abby asked. She wasn't sure the child understood the question because she answered in Hawaiian. Abby shook her head. "I . . . can't understand your language."

"She says you break *kapu*." Kini came out from behind a nearby hut. His words—though whispered—were frightening. But of all the villagers, he alone had returned to explain. "Your shadow touched *ali'i*—our chief. That mean you steal *mana*, his power. For this, you pay. Luke figure it out. He saw our people bow down in village. He run fast to pool. He try to warn you. Then he fight *kahuna*. That be bad. Very bad."

Terror spread through Abby. She could barely breathe.

Kini looked away, anguished at what he had to say. "You be punished much. In past, some people be killed for such." Kini's eyes were filled with sorrow.

The chills at the back of Abby's neck raced down her spine. The ember of fear in her belly leapt into a roaring bonfire of terror. She felt as though she were suffocating. "You have to help us, Kini! You're our friend!" When Kini's eyes betrayed his fear,

Abby pleaded. "Please, Kini. At least free Luke. It was me who broke *kapu*—he just tried to help me!"

Kini shook his head violently. He reached for Niha's hand. "Mako say anyone who help you escape be hunted down by dogs. Mako kill them. I *see* him kill!" Kini's voice got louder with each word. "He *kahuna nui*, spirit leader. There be nothing I can do! *Nothing!*"

He yanked Niha away. "I sorry." Then he turned and fled, dragging Niha behind him.

Tears welled up in Abby's eyes. Poor Kini! *So* full of fear, he was not free either!

She squirmed against the rough coconut-husk rope that bound her tightly to the stake. Uncle Samuel's words kept coming back to her: Hawaiians had never killed a foreigner for breaking *kapu*. Yet it sounded as if Mako might be planning to do just that. Could it be possible?

Abby searched Luke's face for clues. Yet, even from fifty feet away, she knew he had heard the conversation. She could tell by the way he slumped.

He knows he's going to have to pay for fighting the priest. And it's all my fault.

God, she prayed silently, *please help Luke.* Tears welled up and spilled over her brown spiky lashes. She choked on a sob. *It's not fair. . . . Please help him, God. He's been so mad at You since his parents died. Give him something, Lord . . . something to hang on to.*

Chapter Twelve

Night enclosed the subdued village. Although men came from their huts to stoke fires for the evening meal, none looked their way. When the women came out to tend the cooking, they, too, avoided Abby and Luke.

Abby found the silence unnerving. Her sense of isolation and hopelessness deepened with the color of the sky.

Luke, so far away and tied to his own stake, hung his head in a hopeless gesture. Her heart stricken, she wondered what he was thinking. *Oh, Luke, I'm . . . sorry. So sorry I got us into this.* Tears pooled and spilled, leaving tracks on her dusty cheeks.

She hiccuped with the gasps that had started up. There was nothing left to do but pray before tomorrow's sunrise—and wonder what punishment might await them.

Then a figure darted out of the trees toward her.

"Kini," Abby whispered as he approached her.

"Abby," he began, but then he stopped speaking.

He slowly took off a lei of pink plumeria and put it over Abby's head. Then he bent forward and gently rubbed his own blunt nose against hers, the Hawaiian way of showing affection. "Niha helped me make lei." Abby could see that the lei was a bit skimpy in places, but she appreciated the thought behind it. Its sweet fragrance scented the night air. Kini turned to go, but Abby cried out, "Wait!"

Kini paused and bent down to look her in the eyes. "What, Abby?"

"Kini, you know we didn't mean to break *kapu*. Please help us!"

The young boy looked around fearfully, as if he were worried that someone might have overheard. He shook his head without a word and hurried toward Luke.

He placed another lei over Luke, who looked like he didn't appreciate having his nose rubbed and was just about to tell Kini that. "Ah, never mind," Abby overheard Luke say. Then he stared up at the young boy who had become their friend.

"Kini, you *have* to at least free Abby. She doesn't deserve this!" Abby overheard Luke's fierce and intense words, as if he could will Kini to do the right thing. "Abby's worth it, even if I'm not."

But Abby saw Kini straighten and back away. "They move you tonight to temple. Mako say people no want to see your sad faces. So they put you in pit." A dog barked, and Kini jumped.

"Good-bye—*aloha*." With that, he ran away before he was caught.

The sweet scent of plumeria wafted upward from her lei. Abby closed her eyes and breathed it in. It reminded her of her mother's lilac water and how much she wanted to see her ma, pa, and even little Sarah. Her heart thudded against the wall of her chest. Night had fallen and with it her last hope— that Kini might somehow find the courage to free them.

Lord, I'm so afraid, she prayed.

In a still, small voice, Abby heard Him speak. *ASK AND IT SHALL BE GIVEN TO YOU.*

"Oh, Lord," she whispered aloud to the very real Presence surrounding her, "I need You. . . . please be my refuge."

Some time later, a man came and untied the rope binding Abby to her stake, but he used it to bind her hands securely behind her back. Another *kane* with a torch did the same to Luke. As they marched Abby and Luke into the forest, she was glad to move her stiff limbs. She turned to see Luke but couldn't read his face in the night shadows.

Half an hour later, they reached the end of the trees and came into a clearing that overlooked the pounding sea. Many rocks were piled into an altar, capped with a stone idol. Four thick posts were set in four six-foot-deep holes. A long, gray shark was lying beside two of the pits. One of the men led Abby to the third pit, while the other led Luke to the last pit.

Just before her captor pushed her into the pit, Abby turned and yelled, "I love you, Luke!"

Since he was fifteen feet away, she couldn't read his expression, but his words sounded choked. "You, too, Ab."

"Luke," she called again, "don't forget God. No matter what happens."

Just then Luke's captor grunted and pushed Luke into his pit. Then he wrapped the rope around the log post and tied Luke securely in. Abby's guard followed his lead and threw her roughly into her pit. Red dirt smeared her face and clothes as she fell in feet first beside the upright log. Peering upward, Abby watched the *kane* tie her rope to the log. *If only my hands hadn't been tied behind my back,* she thought wildly. *If only they'd been tied in front, then maybe I could've inched my way up the log.*

Her face had been scraped against the rough log, but she barely felt it as she prayed desperately, *Oh, God, send us an angel—an angel like You sent Peter when You helped him escape jail!*

Then the men tromped away. In a moment all she could hear was the distant ocean pounding the rocky shore. Apparently, they'd been dumped there at least until dawn. But what was Mako planning for them? Far off in the distance, the sound of beating drums began to fill the air.

When Abby heard a furtive scraping sound overhead, she looked up. Kini was staring down at her. Stretching his thin arm far over the opening, he leaned against the upright log. Then something flashed above her. *Luke's knife!* Now Kini leapt down into the pit and cut through the rope binding her. He had come to rescue them after all!

"Kini, you angel!" Awe and gratitude shot through her. *Thank You, dear Lord.*

"Mako very angry. We leave quick," he said. "You climb out?" He went first and then helped pull her out.

Abby gave him a fast hug, and then the two ran to Luke's pit. Kini cut Luke's ropes with shaking fingers. In a split second Luke had jumped out of the pit and was grabbing them both.

"Let's go, Kini," Luke said. He wound the rough hempen rope into a coil and slung it over one shoulder. "We might need this later. Now, which way?"

"You follow," Kini said as he picked up their satchel, which he'd also brought along. Then he began a sprint that led them far from the temple site and along the cliff top.

Chapter Thirteen

Not long after their escape from the pit, Luke gripped Abby's hand. She had started to fall behind. "Run, Abby!" he urged.

"I'm trying," she gasped, as she hurried after Luke, trying to leap over small boulders in the inky night. Her legs were beginning to feel heavy and wooden. She knew that soon she'd be stumbling, falling, and slowing them down even more.

They stopped for a moment to catch their breath on a cliff overlooking the sea. "Moon rises," Kini said quietly.

Luke glanced at the skinny lad. "Thank you, Kini, for rescuing us. That took a lot of courage." He pumped Kini's hand passionately.

"Kini glad to help. We hurry to caves," Kini replied. With that brief breather, they were off again, this time heading downward, slipping on dirt and rocks and leaving a trail for anyone to follow, Abby thought grimly. She wondered when the men would discover that they were gone and begin hunting for them. She knew it was only a matter of time.

After another hour of racing along the cliffs, Kini led them into a forest, which slowed them down.

"We go through trees on way to caves," he explained.

Abby threw herself onto a log, breathing hard. "I can't go on . . . have to rest." Her legs were shaking from exhaustion. "Go on without me. I'm slowing you down."

"No. We won't leave you," Luke said firmly. In the moonlight Abby saw a muscle twitch in Luke's jaw as he grimaced. She knew he would have pressed on if it weren't for her. "We'll rest here for a bit," he said. "Chances are no one knows we've gone yet."

Kini looked like he was about to say something but thought better of it. Instead, he nodded. "Yes, we rest a little."

Abby didn't need to hear the word *rest* twice. She scooted down onto the ground and leaned against the log. Untying the laces of her boots, she rubbed her aching feet and ankles for a few minutes while Kini and Luke whispered about plans. Then she fell into an exhausted sleep.

"Abby, wake up!" She jerked awake at the sound of Luke's voice. Why was he shaking her so hard?

"Do you hear the drums? They've discovered our escape sooner than I thought—and they've got hunting dogs!"

Abby heard dogs baying in the distance as she eyed Luke's, then Kini's, terrified faces. "They come!" Kini cried. "They hunt us!"

Abby pushed herself up and groped blindly for the satchel. Kini had already shouldered it, and Luke had tossed the coiled rope over his head.

She pulled on her shoes and despaired as she fumbled with the laces, knowing she was slowing them down . . . knowing she couldn't run fast enough for them to get away! When her left boot lace knotted, Abby whimpered in panic and pushed the laces inside the boot. She bounced up to follow wherever Luke ran—hoping that the boot would just stay on.

Luke didn't waste a minute. Grabbing her by the hand, he jerked her rapidly through the trees toward the ocean. He explained as they ran. "Kini says if we get into the water, the dogs won't follow. . . ." Luke continued to drag Abby as fast as her legs could go. "They know the island better than we do, but at least we have Kini. Otherwise we wouldn't stand a chance!"

Dear God, Abby prayed, *don't let me slow them down so we get caught!*

Then she concentrated on running. The rest had refreshed her, but she knew it wouldn't take long for her weak legs to buckle. When her ankle twisted on a rock in the dark, Abby went down. She choked back a sob at her scraped knees. "Go on! I'm slowing you down!"

"No, Ab." Luke sounded determined. Helping her up, he put an arm around her waist. Small but valiant Kini moved in and put one arm around her other side. She was practically lifted as they hurried forward. She limped as fast as she could, flinching with pain at every step. But she could hear the drums now, coming closer! When Abby turned back to look, she saw torches on the distant slope above them! The baying of the dogs grew louder.

Tears squeezed out of Abby's eyes as she tried to hurry. They didn't have enough light and didn't know exactly where they were going. Kini was supposed to be in the lead, but he'd fallen back to help Abby. Now he stopped to survey the area, and Abby realized he wasn't sure which way to go. He pointed to the right and motioned for them to head downhill. Too late, Kini discovered that the hillside ended in a cliff some twenty feet away. They could hear waves crashing fifty feet below.

Kini let go of Abby and rushed forward, looking over the cliff. He hurried back. "We trapped," he said, panicked.

The dogs scented their prey and began to howl even more passionately, as if ready to close in on them. Luckily, the *kanaka* were not as fast as the dogs.

"Stay here, Ab," Luke ordered. As he and Kini moved away from her, Abby's heart tightened.

"Don't leave, Luke," she pleaded. She had wanted him to save himself, but being left to face the dogs and crazy Mako alone terrified her.

"Don't worry, I'm right here," Luke said, returning. He held a stout tree branch in his right hand. He dropped the rope where he stood. "We'll make our stand here."

He'd come back to defend her with a tree branch! "Oh, Luke," Abby said, her voice thick with emotion. He *was* her best friend in life.

"No," Kini ordered, taking Abby by the hand. "We go off cliff."

Luke gave Kini a sideways glance. "No way! We'd be smashed to pancakes."

"And the ocean is full of hungry sharks at night!" Abby gushed.

Luke snorted. "Don't worry about sharks, Abby. The fall would probably kill you!"

Abby sucked in a breath. "Thanks a lot, Luke," she said. "You want us to jump off a tall cliff in the dark?" What if there are rocks below?" She screwed up her face, sure Luke would agree. "What are our other choices?"

"No other choice!" Kini said, shaking his head. "Mako come quick."

The dogs howled closely now.

Abby turned to Luke and stamped her foot. "I hate heights!" But she allowed herself to be led toward the cliff's edge.

Kini gripped Abby's hand tightly, slung the satchel's handles over his neck like a giant necklace, and held out his other hand to Luke.

Luke exhaled angrily. Then he slung the coiled rope over his shoulder and gripped Kini's thin hand in his own large one.

"Now!" Luke yelled, running toward the cliff edge and the night sky. As they raced forward, Abby held her skirt with one hand. Her stomach churned so much with fear she could have thrown up.

When the ground gave way, she felt Luke and Kini pull slightly ahead of her, jerking her forward as they leapt through the air. Then she began falling. Down, down, down she hurtled—through the blackness, her stomach rising to meet her throat. She heard the water pounding. Her legs kicked frantically as the fall seemed to last forever.

Seconds later she hit the sea with a thunderous crash. Her hand clasp with Kini was torn apart. The cool water, tasting of salt, surged around her, tumbling and twirling her.

She plunged so deeply, and her clothes were so heavy, that it took forever to rise to the surface. She fought against the downward pull, churning her legs and arms upward, where her desperate lungs ached to get a breath of air.

As she surfaced, she was slapped in the face with a forming wave, then plunged into a trough. But she was alive! She gasped a breath. Though her legs stung from the hard impact, she was not crushed on the rocks.

Kini swam toward her, his arms moving surely through the sea waves as if he were equally at home there. When he reached her, he tread water. "Follow me to shore. It be not far." Then he turned back out to sea. "Luke! You okay, *haole* boy?"

There was a spluttering and a cough. Kini turned to Abby. "Stay here, I be back." As he struck out toward the sound of Luke's voice, Abby's heart began to race at being left alone in the pulsing sea. She could hear the waves on the beach. Or were they pounding against treacherous rocks? *How far from shore am I?* she wondered. The currents seemed to be sucking her slowly away from where she'd last seen Kini. "Kini!" she yelled desperately.

Kini was soon back with Luke grinning beside him. "Fancy meeting you here," Luke teased.

"Oohh! You scared me!" Abby took a mouthful of salty water for her comment.

Kini chuckled. "But we not smashed dead! We hurry to caves." The three began breaststroking toward shore, though Abby wasn't sure exactly where that was. She followed Kini, trying not to get more than six feet behind. Secretly she was terrified that a shark might appear at any moment, and the fear was consuming much of her energy.

Soon she began to fall behind. Luke and Kini were ten or twelve feet ahead of her, and it was getting harder for her to see them. Only Luke's blonde hair shone slightly in the moonlight. She'd completely lost sight of Kini. His dark hair blended into the color of the sea.

Suddenly Kini's face was beside her, and Abby almost sobbed with relief. She could see the understanding in his eyes. "Abby, lay on back and kick. It save strength. I make sure you go right way." He grabbed her dress sleeve. Abby turned over and began to kick with her legs. Looking up at the stars instead of down at the dark water comforted her. Not long after, Kini released her, and Abby felt sand surging beneath her feet.

Chapter Fourteen

At last Abby, Luke, and Kini had come to the south-western shoreline. Emerging in the pale moonlight onto a small, sandy beach, Abby could see they were surrounded on either side by rock cliffs. Most of the shoreline was a volcanic-rock tidal zone.

Kini led them toward the cliffs on the west side. "Rocks slippery," he warned as he set off over the wet lava rocks that were covered with slimy sea plants. The surf pounded against the stones just ten feet away, and sometimes an extra large wave flooded toward them and sloshed over their feet. Already in wet clothes, Abby shivered as the ocean breeze came in off the sea.

Together the three climbed and edged their way out on a rock shelf. Abby began to wonder where it could possibly lead. Sometimes the incoming waves flooded the area up to her knees, and she had to grip the rock wall hard so she wouldn't be washed away. As they began to maneuver upward, Abby kept her eyes on the rocks at her feet, avoiding holes and cracks as she used her hands to pull herself higher. "Kini," she said, breathing hard with the effort, "where are we going?"

There was no answer, and Abby stared up. Kini had disappeared! Then, in a flash, his head reappeared from inside a cave just above her. "This way!"

Luke followed Abby as she struggled to the cave entrance in the dark. Waves pounded loudly behind her, and the wind blew her hair into her eyes. Abby's wilted lei caught on a rock, but she jerked it free.

She could hear Luke grunt as he climbed behind her. "With any luck," he said, as he climbed into the cave entrance after Abby, "the waves will wash away our scent."

Kini stood deeply inside the cave. "Dogs not come here. Men will, but now tide rises," he said cryptically.

Abby rested on a boulder and looked around. The cave was damp and cool. Water glistened in the dim moonlight on the walls and floor. The pounding of the ocean, so close by, echoed in the cave. After a brief rest, Kini urged them on. "Mako coming. He be more mad than when Queen Regent throw gods into sea. We hurry."

Abby sighed and rose. "Lead on, Kini. We'll follow you anywhere." Just as she started out behind Kini, she uttered a cry.

"What's wrong, Ab?" Luke asked, coming up behind her.

"My lei is gone."

"Don't worry. You can always get another one."

Panic spread across her face. "It's not that. I'm afraid it fell off nearby. If they see it, they'll trace us here."

Luke, whose wilted lei still hung around his neck, put a hand on her shoulder and squeezed. "There's no sense worrying. Let's just get away from here and hope for the best."

Kini was already yards ahead, the wet satchel still adorning his body like a giant necklace. They hurried to catch up. The light dimmed drastically the farther in they went, past boulders, through fissures and twists in the tunnel. And as the sound of the ocean receded, Abby could hear occasional *plinks* of water dripping from the ceiling.

They had been hiking only a short while when the walls narrowed and the ceiling lowered so that they were going to have to crawl. Abby's nose crinkled at the smell of brine that permeated the tunnel.

"Luke, I have my tin box of matches in the satchel. Let's see if we can light the candle." They stopped, their feet soggy in inches of cold ocean, while Kini handed her the satchel and Abby rummaged through it. She found the box and the tiny candle by feel. "If the box was watertight, we might just get a flame going." She tried to dry the candlewick between two fingers. When she opened the tin, she didn't feel wetness on the matches. With slightly shaking fingers, she struck the match. It sputtered.

Luke spoke up. "Try a dry rock, if you can find one." Abby strained her eyes and sighted a couple rocks about shoulder-high that weren't glistening with water. She struck the match against one and smiled when the match flared into a yellow flame. With hands still shaking from adrenaline, she lit the candle and dropped the match in the water below.

Luke reached for the candle, and Kini took the satchel again. As they made ready to head farther in the tunnel, Luke asked, "Kini, it's not that I doubt you, but have you ever been here before?"

In the cramped space, they not only heard one another breathing but also a distant sighing of wind. Kini took a deep breath. "These be singing caves. Kini come here many times, but I not remember this one grow so low." He hesitated. "In dark, I might picked wrong cave."

His voice sounded small and young, Abby thought. She put out her hand and patted his shoulder. "It's all right, Kini. Maybe your grandfather won't know where we've gone, and we'll be able to backtrack soon."

Luke grunted. "One thing's for sure," he said, "we better stay put. To backtrack might mean exposing ourselves to anyone following us. Let's sit tight and see if they come."

Kini groaned in despair, and Abby cringed at the awful position he was now in. "Kini, thank you for rescuing us from those pits. I prayed for God to send an angel, and He did—you!"

"But I break *kapu*," Kini said sadly. "And my parents see me no more. I no more live in my village."

Abby reached for his cold hand. "God promises never to leave us. He'll help you, Kini. He'll help us all."

"We'd better move farther in," Luke said. "Just in case Mako sees your lei and picks this cave." They started up again, bending over painfully as they moved down the tunnel.

But suddenly a low whistle sounded through the tunnel. In several seconds the wind had strengthened into a howling shriek. The candle flickered out.

Abby's heart sped up as the eerie moan funneled around them. But Kini spoke quietly, as if it were commonplace. "Singing caves say tide changing. We go."

"We'll have to crawl," Luke said. "Kini, lead the way."

Abby kneeled down and followed Kini on her hands and knees. Her skirt kept getting in the way and was now soaking up more water from the rock floor. Since it was too dark for anyone to see, she tucked her skirt up a bit and was thankful her pantaloons covered her legs and protected her skinned knee from the hard, wet stones.

Then Luke, who was bringing up the rear, grabbed Abby's boot and gave it a push. "Hurry! I hear voices behind us."

Abby and Kini crawled as fast as they could,

scraping their knees and hands in the rush. Their terror was now as overwhelming as the night around them.

Although the tunnel ceiling got no lower, the walls seemed to close in on them. *Are we heading into a dead end?* Abby wondered. She stopped crawling and turned back to Luke, who bumped her head with his own.

"Ouch." He was breathing heavy from hurrying.

"Should we keep going?" Abby queried. "What if it's a dead end up ahead?"

Luke paused. "Abby, that's a great idea! We'll barricade ourselves in at a narrow point, and they'll think they've reached a dead end. That is, if we can find enough boulders." They immediately began searching the walls with their hands for loose stones and rocks they could use. Abby hated sticking her hands in pitch-black crevices; what if something bit her?

Kini had crawled back to see what was keeping them.

"Kini," Abby asked, "are there snakes here in Hawaii?"

"Sea snakes," Kini answered, "no snake on land. But sea snakes be mean. They chase you and one bite—you die quick." Abby breathed easier until Kini went on. "But in cave, many bad creatures with poison bites to kill you."

Abby drew her hand back and stared in Kini's direction. "Oh, dear."

"Come on, Ab. This is life or death. Collect more rocks." Luke kept moving stones and boulders and piling them on top of one another. But all the movement made noise.

"*Shhh*," Kini insisted, as he kneeled stock-still. They could hear voices, deep male voices. Though they spoke rapidly in Hawaiian, Abby and Luke could clearly hear they were angry.

Luke broke their silence. "Let's go," he urged. "I don't want to wait here for Mako. Maybe this small wall will slow them down." So they again took off on their knees as fast as they could go, scraping skin and bruising shins but hurrying anyway. The ceiling got lower and lower, until Abby almost cried out with fear. *How are we going to get through this?* she wondered as she inched forward on her belly. And then she prayed, *Please, Lord, don't let us be wedged tight underground!*

Just when she thought she couldn't stand it anymore, Kini cried out and Abby heard a splash. She crawled toward the noise and put her hand out, feeling nothing but cool air. "Kini!" she whispered frantically.

"I here," came a voice a few feet away. Abby inched ahead and felt the rim of an opening. She moved forward and swung her legs over the opening, hoping the floor wasn't far below.

"Kini, are you all right?"

"Yes, I be all right." When Abby felt a hand pull on her dangling legs, she got the idea. She let herself slide down the embankment and onto the stone floor of a wide cavern. The inky air had turned a shade lighter, and Abby could now make out Kini's shape and the size of the huge underground room they'd entered. A foot or two of water covered the floor.

Luke came tumbling down through the opening, much like Kini had. "Umph," he grunted with the fall. Then he bounced up and peered around. A whistle of relief escaped him, but seconds later the sound of running water covered it.

"Luke, quick," Kini said, motioning him away from the tunnel hole. "Tide come." As if on cue, a gush of cool ocean water poured out through the opening and pooled in a loud splash at Luke's feet. He jumped out of the way, but soon another gush of seawater erupted from the tunnel, and they hurried away from that spot.

They moved toward the center of the room and sat on some boulders, wondering what would happen next. "Do you think Mako and his men will come through the tunnel?" Abby asked Luke.

"Naw," Luke answered. "The water probably caught them in the middle of the tunnel. I bet they backtracked real fast." He chortled for a moment. "I can see him on his knees getting a cold wave from behind. Bet his feathers are all wet!" He laughed again, then sobered. "But that doesn't mean they won't try again with the morning's low tide."

Abby decided worrying wasn't going to change

anything. At least they had until high tide receded. Meanwhile, she was so sleepy and her legs so worn out that she curled into a ball on the top of the hard granite boulder. "Well," she said with a sleepy sigh, "by then we'll have figured out an escape route."

Chapter Fifteen

Luke was sprawled on a granite rock in the damp chamber on his back. As he snored, his mouth came open, then shut again. Every minute or two a fat water drop formed on the ceiling and fell quickly toward the granite rock, landing with a *plop* on his forehead. When he moved in sleepy irritation, the next drop flew with amazing accuracy and landed in his opened mouth, midsnore, and splashed onto the back of his throat. He coughed, woke, and sat up, dazed.

"What . . . where am I?" he asked groggily. Rubbing his jaw, he looked around the cave and realized that light was streaming in through a crack in the cavern roof some thirty feet away. In the gray dawn his eyes roved over to Abby and Kini, each asleep on a different rock. "Wake up, sleepyheads. We've got gold to find!"

Luke rubbed his hands together to warm them, relishing the thought they were still free and had a treasure waiting out there somewhere for them.

Hope had dawned along with the light shaft that proved there was a way out of the cave.

He jumped down from his rock and landed in three feet of cold seawater. "Ugh," he sputtered, shocked the cave had filled so high. What if they'd been trapped in a low-lying spot with a low roof? They'd have drowned!

At that instant, Abby rolled over—and almost fell into the lake. But Kini shouted a warning, and she caught herself just in time. "Oh, no," she lamented. "Another cold bath before breakfast."

She waded out into the water anyway, joining Kini and Luke, who were already heading toward the light that poured through the ceiling opening. Luke was in the lead as the two waded through the seawater. He was almost standing under the opening when Abby looked down for a second at the swirling waters. When she glanced up again, Luke had disappeared from Abby's sight. "Luke!" she yelled as she tried to hurry through the water toward the spot where she'd last seen him.

"Kini, where's Luke?" Her voice echoed through the cavern. Then up popped Luke's head as he tread water. Kini turned his white-toothed grin on her. "Big hole!" Kini shouted to Abby, who stood waiting as Luke paddled over to where she and Kini stood on the rock floor.

Water dripped from Luke's hair as he stood up. Abby tried to suppress a smirk. "How was your bath?"

He brushed his wet forelock off his face. "Woke me right up—felt good. In fact I think you'd enjoy it." He moved so fast, Abby didn't have time to get away as Luke swung low and scooped her up; then he straightened with her slung over his shoulder. He waded toward the spot where the sunlight shone down through the hole and tossed Abby in. She dipped down, opening her eyes briefly in surprise, seeing dark green water.

She popped back up, her mouth full of salty brine, and spit it out at Luke. He only laughed, but Kini reached out a hand to haul her back onto solid ground. Abby sputtered and wiped wet curls out of her face.

"Thank you, Kini. At least there's *one* gentleman in the group." She smiled at Kini, who actually blushed.

Well, I'll be, Luke thought. Pint-sized Kini has a crush on Abby.

"Now that we've had our fun and games, how do you propose we get out of this, ah, pleasure chamber . . . before company arrives?" she queried.

The two boys looked at each other blankly, then peered around the cavern. The rock walls rose gently, like an inverted bowl, but the opening was at the very top. "There's no way to climb out, is there?" Luke asked no one in particular. Kini surveyed the situation with dismay.

"The rope!" Luke shouted. Sloshing back through the water to the rock he'd slept on, he retrieved his coiled rope. Waves lapped at the cavern sides as he headed toward Abby. Tying a loop in one end, he said, "Let's hope it's long enough."

Abby watched apprehensively. "Oh, I hope, I hope. . . ."

Luke surged out in the water, coming as close to the shaft of light as possible. He inched his foot out until he felt the ledge drop off underwater. Now he was in as good a spot as possible. He swung the rope around like a lariat and tossed it as high as he could. It hit the ceiling close to the opening and then plunked down in the water.

"Close, but no papaya," Kini said. Luke grinned, then swung the rope again and again, hoping it would shoot out of the hole and snag on something nearby . . . a rock, a tree stump, anything that would hold their weight so they could pull themselves out. Again and again Luke tried, often hitting the ceiling. Sometimes the looped end would disappear out the hole into the sunlight. But it wouldn't snag. Luke's arm grew tired after twenty minutes; he eased it up and down, trying to get the ache out. "We might have to backtrack and risk running into Mako," he said, a scowl creasing his forehead.

"Try one more time, Luke," Abby said. "I'm praying."

But Kini waded over to Luke and took the rope from him. "You rest arm." He cocked his head, as if gauging the distance, then swung the rope. On the first try it fell short. But unbelievably, Kini's second try went soaring out the hole into the bright sunlight. Kini whooped.

"It caught!" Abby yelled ecstatically.

Luke grimaced. "Show off," he muttered as Kini yanked hard and the rope held.

Abby waded over to Kini and threw her arms around him. "Great job!" She turned back to Luke. "Do you realize this means we can start hunting for the gold?" She gave him a radiant smile. "Oh, how wonderful! A day ago we were in big trouble. But today we might strike it rich!"

"Dash all," Luke said, trying to catch the jubilant mood. He waded over to Kini and pulled on the rope, half-hoping it would come loose. But it held fast, and Kini appeared downright blissful about it.

"I climb out, Luke." With that, Kini retrieved the satchel and slipped the handles over his head again. He gripped the rope tightly and swung above the water over the deep hole. The sunlight hit his shoulders as he climbed hand over hand up the rope.

"Wow," Abby said, impressed, "he's quick. You'd never guess such a skinny kid could do that so well."

"What do you expect?" Luke said, irritated. "He's been climbing coconut trees all his life. Jumping off fifty-foot cliffs and dragging me with him!"

Abby looked confused. "Well . . . that's good, isn't it?"

Luke scratched his head and then said, "I guess so, Abby." They were so busy talking they didn't see

Kini climb through the opening at the top. When they next looked up, he'd disappeared.

Luke then gripped the rope in the same way and started up it. "Follow after me, Abby, and we'll be on our way to the treasure."

"I'm not good at this kind of thing, Luke," Abby worried.

"You'll do fine," he said. "And if you have trouble," he added kindly, "I can pull you up from the top."

Then, with great effort, he began to pull himself, hand over hand, out of the water. Luke was stronger than Kini but also a lot bigger. He had more weight to manage, so it was slower going. As he climbed higher and higher, water streamed off him and splashed into the pool below. His ropy arm muscles bulged with effort.

Midway he stopped, wrapping one foot around the dangling rope while he took a minute to catch his breath. Then he began again, hand over hand. Abby watched him ascend into the shaft of light.

As Luke neared the top, he again gripped the rope with his feet. This was the hardest part, he realized. Since the rope hung against the ledge, he'd have to let go of the rope with one hand to get a grip on the moist lava-rock ledge. *How'd Kini do it?* he wondered. Just as he stretched out one hand toward the rocks, a large masculine arm reached down into the cave, momentarily blocking the sunlight.

Luke's stomach jumped into his throat with fright. It wasn't Kini's arm—it was too big and pale! And the head that peered into the cave only had one eye. The other was covered by a black patch!

Luke's face turned pale—the freckles almost disappearing—as he looked at the black eye patch and brown moustache shaded by the low brim of a hat.

"Take me hand, son!" the man ordered. Luke was in no position to argue. He reached up, and soon the stranger's strong grip began pulling him through the hole.

As Luke sprawled out in the sunshine on the ground over the cavern, he inhaled deeply. "Who are you?" he questioned, looking up into the face of the man Abby had seen spying on them in Lahaina.

"No time for chitchat," the man replied tersely. "Those natives are out looking for the lot o'ye, and I'd rrrather not tangle with them if we can avoid it." His clipped Scottish accent and rolling *r*s tickled Luke's ears. "Best get yer other friend free from the bog below."

"Right," Luke agreed, immediately sensing this large one-eyed man was a friend, not a foe. But Kini's face registered concern.

Luke leaned down through the hole. "Abby, climb up!"

She swam out to the dangling rope and gripped it with her wet hands, only to pull herself up one or two handholds, then slide back down into the water. Her upper body strength couldn't compare with Luke's or Kini's, and Luke could see her frustration mount. Luke and the stranger consulted quickly and decided to let down the rope's looped end, which Abby could sit in. They'd pull her up.

As Luke bent down through the ceiling to explain to Abby what they were doing, he caught sight of a white streak in the water near her. It moved again, and Luke sucked in his breath. "Kini," he asked, poking his head back up in the sun, "those sea snakes, what color are the poisonous ones?"

Kini's eyes grew serious. "Bad ones are white and black rings. Why you ask?"

"Because I think one's swimming next to Abby!"

Luke's head plunged through the hole and he hollered at her, "Take the loop, Ab, and sit in it! Quick now, we haven't got all day." *Should I tell her about the snake that's swimming four feet away from her, or will it just scare her?* "Abby," he said, making up his mind, "watch out for that snake on your left."

When Abby looked over, a scream exploded from her that echoed through the cavern and hurt Luke's ears. "Sit in the rope, Abby! We'll pull you up!" He could see her terror as she watched the snake slither straight toward her in about three feet of water.

Abby threw the loop over her head and sat in it. Luke yelled, "Pull!" The rope jerked rapidly, knocking Abby's legs out from under her and dragging her through the black seawater, straight toward the banded snake!

"Hurry!" she screamed. Her legs streaked by the snake, and it turned as fast as lightning back toward her. Then Abby was hauled upward, and the snake got a swift kick in the head from Abby's wet leather boot. As she was yanked several feet out of the water, the snake twirled on the surface, hunting for her. But it only found water droplets raining down from her wet clothes as she was lifted toward the ceiling. The rope jerked her with each movement from the boys and the stranger until she reached the top. Then Luke's hand gripped hers, and he pulled her through the opening and onto safe, dry ground.

Abby looked around. "Thanks, gentlemen." She swallowed, unsure, when she saw the mysterious man with the eye patch and hat. "You were chasing us on Maui."

He nodded. "The name is Duncan MacIndou. I was hired by Dagmar Gronen to find Luke and bring him home." He twirled his brown handlebar moustache and gazed at the object of his hunt. "I followed ye on the next ship leaving San Francisco, Luke. Mrs. Gronen knew ye'd gone with the Kendalls—but it took me awhile to find them. By the time I got to Samuel Kendall's ranch, ye two had left. When I reached Kailua, I learned which ship ye'd taken."

He toyed with his dark moustache, then continued. "I caught sight o'ye in Lahaina, then realized ye'd taken that rusting hulk to Lanai. O' course, I wasn't sure where ye'd disembarked. But last night when I saw torches and heard the dogs, I followed. I saw the three of ye leap off that cliff. What a sight that was!" The stranger laughed lustily, one eyebrow cocked at Luke. "Hope ye don't take it in mind to do that again. I'm not keen on jumping off cliffs."

Then he sobered. "Luke, are you having too good a time to go home?"

Luke kicked a plant with his toe, then said, "California's not home." Luke looked thoughtful for a moment. Then he continued, "I'm sorry Mr. MacIndou, but I think you've come all this way for nothing. We're out to complete our mission. We're not leaving until we do."

"Then, Luke, it appears ye'll have a Scotsman on yer tail until ye do, for I take me work seriously as well. So tell me, what is this grand mission yer on?"

Luke gave Abby a questioning glance. He knew she wouldn't want the one-eyed man to learn about their treasure. He might want it! Luke scanned the pistol and knife hanging on the man's belt. The Scotsman looked unshakable, committed . . . but he didn't look ruthless like Jackal.

Then Abby cleared her throat. "We're on a treasure hunt, Mr. MacIndou."

The dark eyebrow above his black patch arched. "Is that so, now? And did ye get the map from a genuine pirate?"

"As a matter of fact," Luke said eagerly, "we did!"

Abby tapped her foot impatiently. "You're welcome to join us. But first we've got to get away from Mako, Kini's grandfather, and . . . we're not leaving without that treasure. My family needs it. And we've lost all kinds of time since being captured. . . . On top of that, there's a very bad man named Jackal who might also be hunting the treasure. So we've got to get to it before he does."

The stranger's one steel gray eye showed amazement, but Abby plunged on. "So, if you're joining up with us, you need to know we're not splitting the gold. It goes to my pa. But pretty soon Mako is going to discover we're not in the cave, so we need to head out."

"Thank ye fer the invitation . . . and the rules," the Scotsman said, his face strained as if he were trying not to laugh at Abby's determination. He twirled his handlebar moustache absently. "Gold hunting is a favorite pastime o' mine. Since we'll be mates, please call me Duncan."

Abby nodded and wiped her forehead in the hot sun. Luke bet she wished she hadn't left her bonnet behind in the village. *He looks skeptical about the gold,* her eyes seemes to say, *but he won't be for long!*

Then they all took off up the coast, where hidden treasure waited.

Chapter Sixteen

As they hiked, Abby had time to note that Duncan's silver pistol had a black dragon on its handle. He also carried a goatskin water bag and a small pack on his back. He'd obviously been trekking over land to find them since arriving on Lanai, but his hair was neatly combed and his moustache trimmed. In short, even though he was over six feet tall, and most of it muscle, he looked the part of a gentleman on a stroll through the wilds. But he was no frilly, ring-wearing dandy with a starched collar. He'd told them he'd spent six years in London as a private detective and had only recently come west to see new lands.

"I've always wanted to travel to the famous Pacific Islands," he explained, "and yer aunt provided the perfect job and funds fer me to do so. Course, I could see she is a shrewd businesswoman, Luke. I had a hint of why ye'd left, but she's yer only relative, lad. That counts fer something."

They hiked a good hour, which was a trial for

Abby, but the time went quickly as Duncan filled them in on how he'd seen them enter the cave. "When I saw the *kanaka* follow you, I hoped the cave was an empty lava tube. If it was, I figured it probably ran inland in a pretty straight line. So I followed it backward and hoped ye kids would find another exit. At the very least," he said, "if the *kanaka* found you, then I'd probably hear all the hullabaloo." He twirled his moustache. "And I was prepared to rescue ye from them."

Then Duncan shared a few of his exploits tracking people in London, and before long they had grown comfortable with each other. Abby still worried about Duncan seeing their treasure. But there was no help for that now. For better or worse, Duncan was a part of their gang.

As they hiked along, Duncan asked questions, "to prepare meself fer what might occur," he said. "Who is this very bad man who might also be after the gold?"

"His name is Jackal," Abby answered. "And he's a varmint from the word *go.* He's the one who led the mutiny against Captain Chandler—a nicer man you couldn't find."

Luke jumped in. "You see, Abby stole his treasure map after she whacked him on the head with a peppershaker and he passed out. Had a doozy of a headache, I imagine. Then, when we captured Jackal, Abby dropped his treasure map in the sea while he was watching. You shoulda seen his eyeballs pop out of his head. . . . But she was too smart for him. See, she'd made a copy of the map, and we have it right here," he said, pointing to the satchel he'd traded off with Kini and was now carrying.

Duncan eyed Abby appreciatively, then took off his hat with a flourish and bowed low to her. "Yer ladyship, yer courage has made ye the queen of me hearrrt." Luke snorted, Kini laughed, and Abby grew pink in the cheeks.

"That's how they do it at English court," Duncan explained, putting his hat back on. "The bowing, I mean."

Abby's eyes glowed with curiosity. "You've been to court? The English court with the queen?"

By now everyone had decided to take a much-needed break in the shade of a stand of trees. Duncan nodded in answer. "Only once, yer lady-ship. I didna meet the queen that day, but I did find an answer to me question."

"What was your question, Duncan?"

"I sought information about me father, who'd disappearrred when I was just a wee lad. I discovered the name o'the ship he'd taken to America. And I've been following that lead ever since."

Duncan unstopped his goatskin bag and offered Abby the first sip of water. "Thank you, Duncan," she said as she tilted the unwieldy bag up and tried to squirt a stream of liquid in her mouth. It hit her in the eye, bringing chuckles from Kini and Luke. When Luke got some in his ear, Abby giggled unmercifully. But the lighthearted banter felt as though they were truly comrades in adventure. "Probably the first time ye've washed yer ears in a month o'Sundays," Duncan teased.

Abby untied her satchel and extracted the map from her journal. She smoothed it out on a rock in the sun. They all gathered around to try to determine where they were. Everyone looked at the spot marked *X*, which had smeared from the dousing it had recently encountered. Anticipation rose as they realized they must be close.

"So, we're looking fer a small bay that has a large banyan tree inland just a bit. . . ." Duncan took an expert drink from the goatskin bag and restopped it. He rose and slung it over his shoulder. "Let's head up over the next rise. It could be just the other side of it." Then he turned to Kini. "Have ye come this far before, lad? Does yer family use this area?"

Kini nodded vigorously. "Yes, *wahine* come here for star fruit *mauka*, 'toward mountain,' and sometimes go *makai*, 'to beach,' beyond here. There be sea grass for lei. There is small bay."

Duncan grinned. "There's yer answer, Abby. This could be it. Lead away, Kini." On the downhill hike Duncan shared more of his life with them. "When me dear mother died, I was quite young. Me poor father had loved her desperrrately and couldn't abide staying where memories o'her hurt so much. He took me to me aunt's in Glasgow and set off himself fer adventures on the sea.

"I always thought he'd eventually return to get me." Duncan shook his head and continued. "There be rumors that've come back to me, though I don't know whether to believe them, about him making it to these islands."

"I wonder why he'd come," Abby mused, "all the way from Scotland."

"No doubt it was the tales of warmth and a land o'plenty. But he's been missing fer many a year. I imagine he's dead and gone. Still, hearing he made it this far made me always aim to get here—to pick up his trail," he explained. "I cannot help but think I may discover something about him, something I'll be glad to know. I've missed him and me mother."

Luke, who'd lost both his parents almost four years earlier, met Duncan's gaze with genuine sympathy. As Abby watched, something passed between them—a recognition of what such a loss is like, and perhaps a bond. It was at that moment Abby knew Duncan would somehow be an important part of Luke's life.

Kini broke into the conversation. "We best go quick. Mako not give up easy."

They mounted the top of the next rise in only twenty minutes and stood overlooking a tiny beach. Lush vegetation grew down close to the sand. "There must be a creek, with all that greenery," Luke said.

"Fresh water there," Kini answered, pointing. He led the way as they headed down the hill and into the forest that surrounded the bay. As Abby's weary legs propelled her toward her goal, her heart began to lighten. *We're so close! This very day we might be digging up mounds of diamonds, jewels, gold coins. There's bound to be enough to pay off Duncan, so he doesn't take Luke home . . . I hope. And then Kini can come back with us to Oahu, and we'll all live together forever! I'm never leaving home again.*

When Abby tripped over a vine, she stopped daydreaming about gold. "Keep a lookout everyone," she advised. "We could pass that banyan tree anytime now."

They walked downhill for some time and then the land flattened out. Soon they came upon a small clearing. As they walked out into it, Abby gasped. There in the center grew a giant banyan tree. From this distance, they could see its roots rising up from the ground like frozen water geysers that branched upward with foliage. Banyan trees, Abby had learned from Uncle Samuel, sent suckers up out of the ground. The suckers then grew into limbs. This tree was immense, covering about thirty feet.

"There's our banyan," Luke said with a whistle.

Duncan nodded. "The puny one in Lahaina can't comparrre to this beauty."

They drew closer, their hearts beating fast because they were sure this was the *X* on the map. Now all they had to do was circle it and decide on the right place to begin digging.

"I knew we should have brought a shovel," Luke lamented.

Abby was already ahead of him.

But as she hurried forward, hope spreading across her face, she let out a shriek of dismay. The ground around the banyan tree was dug up. "Someone's beat us to the treasure!"

Chapter Seventeen

Abby raced around the tree, kicking the loose dirt clods that had been overturned by someone else's shovel. She scrambled about frantically, but finally reality hit home.

"The treasure's gone. Someone stole it!" She sat down hard on one of the tree's gnarled roots. There would be no rescuing of her uncle's ranch. They were going to remain poor. All she and Luke had gone through was for nothing!

The anticipation that had been physically sustaining Abby evaporated. She put her head in her hands, her legs suddenly too weak to go any farther. "Oh, Luke. What are we going to do? How will we ever survive without that money?" She tried hard to hold back the tears.

Duncan stroked his moustache silently. Luke shook his head sadly, kicked the sandy soil, and plopped down in the tree's shade three feet away from Abby.

Dropping his pack and goatskin water bag,

Duncan investigated the area carefully. He bent down and picked up a large dirt clod, turning it in his massive hands.

Abby looked up, her face despairing. "What are you doing, Duncan?" What she really wanted to say was, *What could you possibly find interesting about a piece of dirt?*

Duncan turned the earthen clod one more time, then dropped it. "Collecting clues. This dirt was turned within the last few hours. It's not quite drrried out yet." Then he continued walking about the site.

"I'm going to that creek we saw from the hill. I need to cool off," Abby said, exasperated. She glared at all of them, fully intending them to get the message to leave her alone. She'd rarely felt this grouchy and angry.

Duncan spoke up as she headed toward the trees. "I'm not sure ye should, Abby. Whoever dug this up could still be around."

Abby pinned him with blazing eyes. "No one in his right mind would spend a second longer on this island than he had to. Someone beat us to the trea-sure. You can bet he's long gone! He's probably in Lahaina, buying every sailor in the bar a drink!" Then she flounced off in a huff.

Looking puzzled by Abby's swift change of mood, Duncan queried Luke, who shrugged and said, "Hope she doesn't run into Mako. She'd bury him alive."

Kini sighed. "Grandfather angry man. He still beat Abby if he find her." He sat down now, too. "I will miss my family when we go . . . even little Niha." He shook his head as if he couldn't believe he'd said that.

Duncan twirled his handlebar moustache with his thumb and index finger. "Men, it's time for tea. But since we haven't the right accoutrements, I suggest a nap to enerrrgize our spirits before we make new plans."

Without a further word, they each picked a root on which to lay their heads. The atmosphere was somber, their hearts dejected. One by one, they closed their eyes and began to doze in the midday warmth.

The anger that had motivated Abby's walk to the creek was gone now, and sadness had taken its place. Her eyes were bright with tears of disappointment as she headed toward the sound of running water. *I've failed. Ma and Pa are up a creek without a paddle, and I almost had the treasure that would've changed our lives. Someone beat us by just a few hours!*

She broke through a stand of kukui trees and saw the shallow creek in a golden, sandy bed. The sun filtered through the limbs and dappled the ground and water. A bird flitted from a nearby branch, then swooped over the creek bed with the whirring of feathers in flight.

Abby breathed in the scent of wet earth and shade. She bent down and untied her boots, then sat on a rock and took them off. She waded into the cool water, dipped a palm in, and splashed her face. It felt good and clean, not salty and sticky like seawater when it dried. She waded upstream aways and then saw a green bubbling pool that filled a depression in the creek bed. It was too inviting to ignore, and Abby hurriedly peeled off her top layer of clothes, leaving them on a rock in the sun. They'd be nice and warm to return to.

As she waded out into the pool in her thin undergarments, she shivered. The water was cold but refreshing. She dove under and came up with her long cedar-hued hair trailing behind like silken seaweed.

After ten minutes of diving and swimming, Abby didn't feel as discouraged. She swam awhile longer, reveling in the bracing water, and then sat in the sun to dry. Her hair fell in long ringlets down her back. Admiring the beauty around her, she knew she should pray about the situation and ask God for a new direction. But she couldn't bear to think about it anymore.

An hour passed before Abby felt she could go back and join the men . . . and face the future without a treasure.

She had grown lazy and warm in the sun; now she stood and stretched. *Time to face reality,* she thought, as she dressed and began retracing the steps that had brought her to the pool.

Luke turned over in his sleep, unintentionally bringing his face from shade into full sun. The light pierced blindingly through his closed lids, waking him. But he didn't open them yet—not until he felt hard metal pressed against his chest. His eyes flew open in shock. The blackbearded face of Jackal grinned down at him!

"Rise up slow and easy, boy." The stench from Jackal's rotting teeth washed over Luke. Holding his breath, Luke looked down at the pistol pushed against his breastbone. Slowly, his heart pulsing like hummingbird wings against his ribs, he inched up to a sitting position.

"Where's that troublesome girl?" Jackal asked, his bushy brows meeting over his sharp nose.

Luke swallowed hard, hoping Jackal didn't notice

he had a lump in his throat. He tried to sound calm. "She's not with us." It was the truth; Abby had left some time ago. *Stay away, Abby!*

Jackal smirked. "Ye finally got smart, eh, boy? Left the bad-luck girl out of the picture? Well, yer still outta luck!" His laugh was low and menacing. Jackal then stood and pointed the pistol at Luke's gut. "Go wake the others—real slow-like."

Luke rose quietly and walked to Duncan first. He bent down and gripped Duncan by the shoulder blade. The man instantly woke and leapt up. Jackal cackled, his dry lips splitting into a contemptuous grin. "Sleepin' beauties miss the early worms," he said.

Duncan gaped in astonishment. Luke could tell from Duncan's swift evaluation—of the gun now aimed at his belly, of Jackal's dirty clothes, silver earring, and uneducated words—that Duncan knew this had to be the low-life mutineer the kids had told him about.

Jackal glared at Duncan. "Keep yer trap shut," he ordered, "and wake the little varmint." Luke headed toward Kini, but Kini had already awakened and was sitting up, rubbing his eyes.

"Luke?" Kini asked, as Luke squatted beside him.

"It's all right, Kini. This is someone we've met before—Jackal. Pretty soon he'll realize we don't have what he's looking for and will let us go."

Jackal's mouth curved into a sneer. "Don't have it, eh?" He walked over to Duncan and held out his free hand even as he trained his pistol on Kini. "Give me the pistol, easy-like, or the boy will feel a breeze between his eyes."

Duncan didn't doubt Jackal's sincerity. He slowly reached into his holster and removed the black-and-silver pistol, handing it to Jackal by his one finger on the trigger guard. Jackal grunted. "Turn around." When Duncan did, he raised the gun and whacked him soundly on the back of the head. Duncan lurched, then fell to his knees before he passed out.

"What'd you do that for?" Luke hollered, jumping up. "We don't have the treasure. We thought you had it. Someone does—the ground's all dug up!"

Jackal's eyes squinted, roaming over Luke and Kini, as if they might be hiding something on their persons. "I did the diggin', and there ain't nothin' here!" His face burned with blotches of anger. "I risked me life to get back here, and I ain't leavin' without the gold, ye got it?" He waved the gun at Luke and Kini, weaving it back and forth carelessly.

Luke bent down to see to Duncan's wound. Blood oozed out, but Duncan was beginning to stir again.

Storming over to them, Jackal kicked Duncan in the side, sending him into a spasm of pain and groaning. "Git yer backs against the tree!" he ordered. "If'n ye ain't gonna tell me where the treasure is, ye can rot here for all I care." With that, the three sat down against the banyan's bark and submitted to the rope tying as Jackal walked around the tree, wrapping them in a web that pressed their hands tightly against their chests. When Jackal was through, they were forced back against the trunk, with little chance of escape.

As Abby neared the clearing, she heard an angry voice. Crouching down, she moved forward, kneeled behind a large fern, and parted its fronds slightly to get a view of the banyan tree. She thought she recognized the voice, but she didn't dare believe it. Now, as she saw someone pacing back and forth waving two pistols, Abby's pulse began to race. It *was* Jackal!

She wanted to run—in the other direction. She knew he'd kill her with his bare hands if he could. If he took the treasure, why didn't he leave? As she wondered, images of Jackal fighting in the streets of Lahaina flooded her memory. He'd enjoyed kicking his opponent when he was down. Then she remembered him promising to sell her into slavery. And another picture popped into her head—when she'd dropped the map into the sea, Jackal had stared at her with murderous eyes. "I'll git ye, ye stupid girl!"

Abby moved closer to Jackal until she thought

she could smell his stench coming downwind—the bad breath and sweaty clothes. Or was it just her memories and fear? Gulping a breath, she inched closer until she could clearly see the banyan tree. *There's Luke, Kini, and Duncan—all tied up!* Jackal stalked back and forth in front of them, talking like a madman.

"Ye'll die of thirst, if'n ye don't give me the treasure. I know ye took it and hid it somewhere else!"

Duncan treated the mutineer as if he'd lost his mind. "That's corrrect," he said sarcastically. "We unburrried the treasure, hid it elsewhere, and then rrreturned here to rrrest—so in case ye showed up, we could explain the situation." Duncan tried to raise his right hand, but it was restrained by the rope tied across his chest. Abby suspected he'd been about to twirl his handlebar moustache, a habit she'd grown used to seeing in the short time she'd known the Scotsman.

Jackal's pupils dilated at the disdainful comment. His black eyebrows hunched over his glittering eyes like evil centipedes. "Ye won't be so uppity in a day or two, when the heat draws all the water from yer body." He stalked over to Duncan and backhanded him across the mouth. "I can afford to wait," he said with a laugh. "The question is, can ye?"

Jackal settled down with a brown bottle of rum. Abby watched his biceps bulge over his rolled-up shirtsleeves each time he lifted his hand to take a swig. The man was all muscle and meanness. Jackal meant to get what he came for, she realized.

Then she, too, settled down to wait—though for what, she wasn't sure.

Chapter Eighteen

An hour later, Abby's legs cramped. Quietly she stretched them out. Jackal had been steadily guzzling rum and had gone from angry outbursts to confused rambling. For the last ten minutes he'd been sleeping several yards away from Luke on one of the banyan's many roots.

Questions had been nagging her. If Jackal didn't have the treasure, who did? And how did he get here? He couldn't have swum, so perhaps he had a boat. She decided to investigate the nearby shore. There she discovered a small sloop with mast and sail neatly folded. So they had a way off the island, if only Abby could free them!

When she returned to check on Jackal again, Abby heard deep snores. She edged toward the tree. I must be careful. If I get caught, we're all done in! *Dear God, help me free Duncan and the boys and get us safely home.*

Fortified by her prayer, Abby edged out from behind the ferns. In the sandy soil, her footfalls were a mere whisper of sound, which the distant ocean waves covered. Looking up, she saw Duncan's one steel gray eye trained on her. A slight smile appeared under his long moustache as if to say, *I'm counting on ye, lassie!*

Abby walked stealthily toward the captives and then tiptoed past the snoring pirate. He lay on his back with the empty bottle on his chest, his mouth slung open and a loud gurgling noise, like a boiling pot, issuing forth with every breath. Abby stopped for a second to gaze down at his opened mouth; she hoped a fly would buzz down his throat as soon as they were safely away. But when his bushy black beard twitched unexpectedly, she hurried toward Luke. This was no time to lollygag.

When she reached him, Luke grinned broadly. Abby traced the ropes to the spot where Jackal had tied them. She tried desperately to untie them, but the ropes were wickedly knotted. Finally Luke whispered in frustration, "Get the knife from Kini!"

"In my pouch," Kini answered to her unspoken question. Then Abby remembered he kept it tucked in the side of his *malo. How smart of Kini to keep it hidden,* she thought as she pulled it free. But the pouch, too, was firmly knotted. Abby bent over it, panic rising in her. How much longer would Jackal sleep? She was their only hope of escape; he must not see her!

As she worked at the knot with clumsy fingers, Abby heard the snoring stop. A tremor jolted through her when she saw Jackal was sitting up, his back to her as he scratched his dirty beard! Her first instinct was to flee. But when she glanced at Luke, he raised his eyes to the lofty banyan tree. It was her only chance, she realized. Running would draw attention to herself, and Jackal was about to turn toward them any second. There wasn't time! In a brief moment of indecision, Abby watched Jackal rub his chin and burp. With growing horror, she knew he was about to get up. Without another thought, Abby stepped on Luke's shoulder with her hard boot heel. Luke sank his teeth into his lower lip to keep from crying out in pain, while Abby flailed silently around, trying to swing herself up into the leafy branches.

Jackal was pushing off on his knees to a standing position just as Abby was launching herself up into the tree's shady interior. As he turned around to view his prisoners, Abby brought her left foot up the tree to stand motionless in the V-shaped trunk. If he happened to look toward her, she realized he'd see her boot, but it was higher than his head and he might not think to look up. So Abby held as still as stone and prayed that God would cover her.

"I be thirsty," Jackal grumbled to no one in particular. He glanced around the spot, as if expecting to see something, then headed straight toward Luke—and Abby right above him. "Not so high and mighty now, are ye, boy?" He looked at Luke arrogantly and aimed a kick at him, but it fell short.

Jackal almost lost his balance. He grunted and stumbled toward an empty wooden bucket. Picking it up, he lurched away toward the creek.

Abby lost no time in rearranging herself as she looked up. A few feet above her grew a stout limb she could perch on, so she moved her feet into position to climb. But just as she did, her right foot slipped down into a depression in the tree trunk, into the V where it branched out in two directions. Abby gasped as she realized her foot was trapped in a large knot-hole. She was stuck fast. *No! This can't be happening!*

As soon as Jackal disappeared, Luke whispered urgently. "You all right?"

"No, I'm . . . stuck in a knot-hole. If he comes back, he'll see me for sure!"

Duncan craned his head to see Abby. "Pull down a branch fer cover."

Abby searched the immediate area while trying to free her foot. It was not going to budge—at least not in the next couple of minutes. Maybe if she undid her laces and yanked her foot out of her boot . . .

She grabbed hold of one limb, as thin as two pencils, and broke it off. The cracking noise rang out loudly, but Jackal didn't reappear. Abby placed the leafy branch over her boot and leg just seconds before the husky mutineer ambled back toward the tree. He was slopping precious fresh water over the sides of the bucket and down onto the dry, sandy soil.

He eyed the men, then took a deep draught of
water, half of it spilling carelessly down his
shirtfront. When he finished, he asked maliciously,
"Water anyone?" He cackled, then took another
mouthful. Abby had always suspected, and now was
sure, that Jackal was a few hay bales short of a load,
for next he threw back his head and gargled loudly.
"Ahhh. That was good on me hot, dry throat." Then
he set the bucket down, right in front of them, and
went about picking up twigs and dead branches. He
threw them down about ten feet away from Luke
and began building a fire for the night.

An hour later the fire crackled, sending up occasional showers of gold sparks as Jackal tossed kin-
dling on it now and then. Abby watched from her
perch as Jackal dug through a sack and took out a
dead chicken. He began looking around, picking up
sticks. Evidently he wanted to roast the chicken over
the fire. He tried several sticks, but they couldn't
hold the weight of the bird.

As Jackal eyed the tree limbs and foliage above,
Abby experienced a moment of sheer terror. But
when he seemed to find what he wanted in a sucker
shoot growing about chest high, Abby relaxed.

It wasn't long before the chicken's fat began to

drip into the fire, wafting up wisps of smoke and delicious odors. Abby's mouth began to water. *Plump, tender chicken breasts,* Abby thought with longing. *I'm starving, and the boys must be, too. I could eat for two hours and not be satisfied.* Her stomach rumbled with pangs of hunger.

When Jackal finally removed the browned chicken from the fire, he blew on a leg. Sinking his teeth into the juicy meat, he groaned in pleasure. Abby turned her face away. She remembered how hard she'd once hit him with Captain Chandler's peppershaker, and the memory helped some.

When he was finished eating, Jackal wandered over to the banyan tree with the carcass of the bird. Abby noted that it still had white breast meat attached to the ribs. He waved it spitefully under each of his captives' noses, sending the aroma closer to Abby as well. They were all mesmerized by it until Jackal's evil laugh erupted, and he walked casually back to his campfire, tossing the bird onto his canvas sack of supplies. "First one who tells me what I wants to know gits to finish it."

But the only one who spoke was a plover who'd come inland to investigate the firelight. With a fast flap of wings, it flew off.

Just then Luke burst into song. "Well, I miss my girlie from Californie," he sang out, and Abby heard Kini giggle. From her vantage point she could see the surprise on Jackal's face, as if he couldn't believe a hungry, thirsty, beaten boy would have anything to sing about. But as Abby heard Luke belt out the words, her heart soared like the plover winging its way back to the sea. There was freedom and determination in the song, as though no evil could kill the spirit of a boy with hope.

Luke sang the ditty through once, and on the second round, Kini and Duncan joined in as best they could. Abby almost opened her mouth, too, she was so caught up in the spirit of it, but she stopped herself just in time. Her arm ached from holding the branch in front of her foot, and her foot had gone numb from its awkward position in the knot-hole. But Luke's voice brought her unexpected joy.

Even Jackal wasn't bothered by the singing. When he pulled out another brown bottle of rum, he lay down in front of the fire, his face toward Luke, and appeared to enjoy the lighthearted tune. The longer he drank, the more jovial he became, until he was actually trying to sing along. Abby sat amazed by it. This was a side to the evil man she'd have never guessed existed. When they'd sung the ditty six times, Jackal spoke up. "What's next, me boys?"

Duncan's rich tenor soared into the night, thrilling Abby with a hymn she'd heard only once before. Its haunting Welsh melody rose through the tree limbs to God Himself:

> *Guide me, O Thou great Jehovah,*
> *Pilgrim through this barren land;*

I am weak, but Thou art mighty—
Hold me with Thy powerful hand:
Bread of Heaven, Bread of Heaven,
Feed me till I want no more,
Feed me till I want no more.

Abby grinned as she listened to Duncan's reference to food. He, too, was hungry! Then his song went on, building Abby's courage as the old hymns were meant to.

Open now the crystal fountain,
Whence the healing stream doth flow;
Let the fire and cloudy pillar
Lead me all my journey through:
Strong Deliverer, strong Deliverer,
Be Thou still my strength and shield,
Be Thou still my strength and shield.

As the last note died away, Abby saw Jackal cap his bottle and get up slowly. She was amazed as she watched him pick up the water bucket and bring it first to Kini, holding it up to his parched lips. Kini drank noisily, water sloshing down his chest. When he'd had his fill, Jackal presented it to Luke, holding it to his lips, too. When Luke had drunk long and deeply, Jackal moved on to Duncan. He paused before bringing it to the Scotsman's lips, then held it steady. When Duncan had drunk, he gazed up at his captor. "Thank 'ee."

Jackal seemed to look through Duncan, as if he were seeing something far away, then spoke. "Me ma used to sing that one . . . a long time ago." Then he went back to his spot by the fire, put down the bucket, and settled down to sleep.

In fifteen minutes the blackbearded rogue was fast asleep, snoring as if he were trying to signal Hawaiians on Oahu. Abby set aside the branch and began working on freeing her foot. She stuck her hand in the side of the hole and tried to feel what it was caught on. A separate piece of wood was lodged inside the knot-hole and jammed above her boot's toe. She scrunched two fingers in the narrow opening and pushed the wood with all her might. When it came free she almost shouted in triumph but was mortified instead to hear the wood piece rattle sharply as it fell against the inside of the tree trunk.

But Jackal kept snoring. Luke, however, peered up into the branches with a worried expression on his face. "Ab," he called softly, "you all right?"

Abby shushed him and stretched out her ankle and leg. "Ahh," she murmured with delight. Her foot had been imprisoned by that wood far too long. She rubbed her foot hard, trying to get the blood back in. She was rewarded when pinpricks of pain speared her as blood flowed to her foot again. Then, out of sheer curiosity, she reached down into the hole to extract the culprit.

As she dug down, she felt the loose piece of wood and pulled it up. Even in the dim light of the campfire, she could see it was not just a dead branch of the banyan tree. It was a carved, sweet-smelling piece of sandalwood—in the shape of a dolphin!

Abby held up the ten-inch carving in wonder and rubbed the animal's smooth sides. Whoever the artist had been, this was clearly one of the long sleek dolphins she and Luke had so recently met—one of the spinners that had befriended them!

In her concentration, Abby didn't notice the tree branch slip out of her lap and clatter to the ground after it bounced off Luke's head. "Ouch." Luke pierced Abby with an irritable glare.

Everyone held their breath as Jackal stopped snoring, rubbed his bearded cheek, and turned on his side, facing them! Then the snores resumed.

It was time to get out of there, Abby realized. But she couldn't help but investigate the knot-hole one last time before climbing down. If someone put a dolphin there, maybe other carvings awaited her. When she plunged her hand in one last time, she drew it back out quickly. She'd touched something soft. Gingerly she eased her hand back into the dark hole and felt the bottom.

Again her fingers touched soft leather, but this time she grasped it and pulled it up. The leather pouch was not big, perhaps a foot long, but it was heavy. It took some maneuvering before Abby could get it out of the hole. When she did, she had to untie the drawstring. What she discovered made her mouth drop open.

Gold and silver coins—doubloons and silver dollars—along with a leather-wrapped package that felt like a book lay in the bottom of the opened bag. Abby's mind registered a noise off in the distance, but her heart was soaring with intense joy. *I've found the treasure!* She looked at the gold gleaming in the meager firelight and her lips spread into a grin. As she held up a fistful of coins, the rest made a clinking sound, and Jackal again snorted and moved. That distant noise began to sound steadily louder.

Abby was startled out of her daydreams when Luke and Kini hissed at her. She gently set the coins back down. *If I don't free the boys, none of us will get to use this!* She couldn't stop to open the leather package. So she stuffed everything, including the dolphin, back inside the bag and retied it. *We all thought the X on the map meant buried treasure, but it meant the gold was hidden in the tree!*

Abby gripped the bag between her teeth as she began to climb down. Now her mind registered what the rhythmic pounding was: *Drums! Mako's coming!*

Panicked, she began to lower herself from the tree, her leg searching through the air for Luke's shoulder. *Luke, I'm sorry!* she apologized silently, as she first stepped on his head, then tried to maneuver her foot onto his shoulder but gently kicked him in his Adam's apple. Luke made a gurgling noise that brought Abby to a halt. But this time Jackal didn't move. How long, however, until the drums and baying dogs woke him?

Chapter Nineteen

Setting the bag down on the ground, Abby tiptoed straight to Kini. Again she began to work the knot on his pouch, but this time her determination worked it loose.

Just as she was pulling out the blade, the drums echoed loudly. Kini's eyes grew round. "Hurry. Dogs be here soon!"

Abby's fingers shook with adrenaline as she sawed the rough rope. *Come loose,* she urged.

Finally the last strands of hemp gave way as the blade cut straight through. Abby hurried to unwind the rope away from their chests—and then Duncan and the boys leapt up.

She handed Kini the knife. "Jackal's boat is down on the beach," she whispered, gesturing toward the skinny path.

Duncan's forehead creased as the distant sounds drew near. "Mako's here! Let's go."

Abby bent down to retrieve the bag of coins with

the carved dolphin inside and tossed it to Luke. "It's the treasure," she whispered.

Mute with surprise, Luke gripped it and followed behind Abby as Duncan and Kini led the way. Just as they were leaving the banyan clearing, Mako's dogs started baying wildly. Jackal rose in confusion, his pistol in one hand and Duncan's tucked in his belt.

"Hurry! Jackal's up!" Luke shouted. A shot rang out, whizzing by Luke's ear, and they broke into a noisy run, leaping over logs, crashing through bracken, and panting in an all-out sprint to the beach.

Jackal was close on their heels. Abby, who had fallen behind, could hear him crashing after them, his voice punctuating the night with curses. She looked back once and saw that he carried a burning branch from the fire to light his way.

Meanwhile, Luke had sprinted ahead to help Kini and Duncan push the sloop into the sea. Luckily it was nearing high tide, and the waves had almost reached the hull. When another bullet sped by Luke, he turned to check on Abby. In horror, he watched her trip over something on the dark beach and go down. Jackal had stopped and thrown down his torch. He was taking aim on Abby when Luke instinctively screamed, "Noooo!" and began racing toward Abby.

Jackal, distracted from Abby, gazed with fascination at the bag Luke held. But he raised his pistol again to eye level, taking aim on Luke.

At that moment Luke launched the bag through the air. Even as Jackal cocked the pistol, the load of coins whizzed through the air and crashed against his left temple. The weapon lowered, and the shot went wild. Jackal stared at Luke through dazed eyes, then fell face-first into the sand.

Abby, only ten feet from Jackal, ran straight toward him. Luke's mouth dropped open. "No! You're going the wrong way!" he yelled.

Abby grabbed the bag and turned back to the water. The sand seemed to weight her feet as she tried to sprint to Luke. He waved his arms frantically at her—or something behind her. "Run!" he screamed. "The dogs!"

She didn't waste time turning to see how close they were, but Luke could see them closing in. Against his better judgment, Luke again ran toward her. He could hear her gasping with effort to get to the boat. Picking up the burning torch Jackal had dropped, Luke brandished it at the dogs that raced onto the beach.

The fire kept the dogs at bay as Abby got to the water and began wading in.

Abby spotted the little sloop sloshing in the waves. Kini was in the bow, working feverishly to hoist the sail, and Duncan leaned toward Abby from the stern. "Come on, Abby!" He held out a hand, and Abby hurried through the waist-high surf with her treasure.

She gripped the bag between her teeth and plunged into the water, waves slapping her in the chest and face. As she started to swim, she turned back to see Luke. He was entering the sea with his back to her, still waving the firebrand at the one snarling dog that had followed him in. It growled and lunged menacingly.

"Luke!" Abby yelled, taking the bag from her mouth, "let's go!" There was no time to lose. Jackal was standing again, and she saw him raise his pistol just before she plunged into the sea.

Luke stood in waist-high water, walking backwards. But when a bullet whizzed by him and hit the wave with a ping, he threw the torch at the canine and dove after Abby.

As Luke began his swim to the boat, Duncan gripped the back of Abby's dress and hauled her in like a caught tuna.

Shivering, she peered back toward shore to see how Luke was doing. She watched in horror as Jackal threw down the pistol—probably Duncan's very own from Scotland—and plunged in after Luke.

Just then Mako and his men flowed out of the trees and onto the beach. Torches lit up the night, and the beating drums thundered out a rhythmic pulse. Abby, soaked but safe, gripped the gunwale of the boat and stretched out a hand toward Luke. "Hurry!"

Duncan was at the tiller, but the little sloop was stalled. Because its sail was not yet pointed into the wind, the waves threatened to push it back to shore—and certain capture. Abby cried out the theme of the song she'd so recently heard Duncan sing: "Help us, O Lord, our shield!"

As Luke clutched the gunwale and began pulling himself up, the boat tilted, managing to turn ever so slightly into the breeze. The sail caught, and Duncan hooted with delight.

Luke fell wet and dripping into the bottom of the sloop, and Abby looked back to see Jackal pound the sea in frustration. He tread water for a moment, shouting curses in Abby's direction. Then he turned to see wild old Mako leaping on shore, pointing and yelling in Jackal's direction.

Abby leaned over to give Luke a hug. "We made it," she said, beaming with relief. The sloop picked up speed.

Luke spit out a mouthful of water, then grinned back. "Yep."

Kini moved over to sit by them. Still at the tiller,

Duncan's face split with delight. He inclined his head back toward shore as the sloop skimmed over the waves and out into the Auau Channel. The kids followed his nod to see Jackal on shore, running away from Mako as fast as his hairy legs could take him. As the line of torches bobbed after Jackal through the dark, Duncan laughed uproariously. "He's getting his just reward."

But Kini, his thin shoulders hunched over dejectedly, was looking wistfully toward shore—and his last glimpse of home.

Chapter Twenty

Duncan and Luke took turns through the night at
the tiller as the wind lulled, then picked up again.
Abby, though eager to examine the leather pouch
full of coins and a book, realized it was too dark to
see much. So she rested in the bottom of the boat.
Without a word, Kini curled up beside her and laid
his head against her shoulder. He'd been quiet since
they'd left the island, and Abby realized he must be
worried about what would happen to him.

"Kini," she said gently as she put one arm around
him, "we want you to come live with us on Oahu.
My parents and Uncle Samuel will be happy to have
you, and I'll be so thrilled to have a brother."

He was silent for a long time. "*Mahalo*," he said
softly. "And then you will tell me more about your
One True God?"

"Yes," Abby said tenderly, as he laid his head in
her lap, the way Sarah often had, and fell fast asleep.

Luke gazed at them. "He's lost his family 'cause

of what he did for us. I wonder if he'll ever see them again."

Abby swallowed the lump in her throat. She'd been facing those same thoughts several hours earlier. Now her heart ached for Kini. "He'll always have a home with us, Luke. We owe him . . . and I already love him."

Then, from the stern, came Duncan's voice. "So, Abby," he asked, "what did ye find in the banyan tree?" When she looked up, she saw Duncan listening quietly from his spot at the tiller.

She smiled. "Gold coins! There's also a book of some kind, but it's too dark to read now . . . and a carved dolphin."

"Can I see the dolphin, lassie?"

"Of course." She opened the leather bag and tossed the wooden carving to him.

He smelled the wood. "It's sandalwood," he commented as he braced the tiller with his arm and turned the dolphin in both hands, stroking the smooth sides and the dorsal fin at the top. "Reminds me of the work me father used to do. He was once a grrreat carver. I remember the tiny animals he carved fer me when I was a wee tyke."

"How wonderful. Do you still have them?" she asked.

"Unfortunately, no. In my profession ye have to travel light. I gave many things away in Scotland." Abby heard him sigh. "I remember me pa prrromised to carve me an elephant—one o'those strange mammoth beasts from India. We'd seen a poster with a drawing of one as we walked through our little village, and I begged him to make me one. But it wasn't long after that me mother died. . . . he never got around to carving it before he left."

There was a long silence. Duncan passed the dolphin back. "Fer many years I believed he'd send me an elephant, to let me know he was thinking o'me. . . . But o'course, one never came."

Abby's heart constricted with Duncan's unsaid words: the intense disappointment one little boy felt in being abandoned after his mother's death. One glimpse at Luke and she realized Duncan's words had impacted him, too.

How lucky I am to have parents, Abby thought. Then she prayed, *Oh, God, thank You. . . . Thank You for helping me get home! And for giving me something to bring home. It's not the huge treasure I'd hoped for, but I've learned, dear Lord, that our times, our money, our very lives are in Your hands. And for that, I'm glad.*

Soon the night was over, and the little sloop skimmed toward Lahaina and the rising sun. The green hills behind the village rose up majestically, and the whitewashed colonial-styled Pioneer Inn looked friendly and civilized in the morning light. With Luke tacking and pulling the boom either starboard or leeward at Duncan's direction, they sailed right into the small harbor. As they drew near the rickety dock, Luke leapt out like an agile cat and tied off the sloop.

"Kini," Abby said with a nudge, "we're here."

He stretched and yawned, grinning at his first sight of Lahaina. Few people were up at the early hour of six in the morning, but no sooner had they disembarked than a balding man with a bulging belly came running from the Pioneer Inn.

"So you've brought back my boat!" he shouted as he hurried toward them barefoot. It looked as though he'd barely taken time to pull on pants and a shirt. His angry face was turning red, right up past his ears to the top of his balding head.

Abby and Luke's mouths gaped open.

It didn't take Duncan long to explain that they had not taken the boat but were willingly returning it. The man's face lost some of its redness as he introduced himself as Mr. Potts, the owner of the Pioneer Inn. Feeling bad that he'd misjudged them, he not only rewarded them with a free breakfast but helped them find passage on a ship bound for Oahu. With the gold Abby had discovered in the banyan tree, she paid everyone's passage but Duncan's. Aunt Dagmar had already given him traveling expense money.

Later that day, as the three-masted *Eagle* got underway, Abby settled in her own tiny cabin and

emptied the leather bag of its treasure. She counted
thirty gold doubloons and twenty-six silver dollars.
Perhaps it would be enough for Uncle Samuel to
buy the ranch.

Then she opened the leather-bound diary and
began to read. Although the owner's name was
nowhere to be found, Abby began to feel as though
she knew the writer. He described the sailing adventure that brought him to the islands. It read:

> August 1814—*Carthagenian* anchored north
> of Lahaina on coral beds. Storm at night
> struck us by surprise, waves fierce, probably
> six-to-eight-foot swells. Anchor loosed and
> ship moved toward Black Rock. All hands
> valiantly raised sails to capture wind, but
> 'twasn't enough time. The *Carthagenian* hove
> into the headland and sunk. Two hands lost.
> The rest made it to longboat, and some swam
> ashore.

> Natives have been helpful. I met King
> Kamehameha today. He was very interested in
> all I could share about my bonnie land and the
> places I ha' been since leaving it. He is a bril-
> liant and witty man. And the size of him! Tall
> and muscled, yet surprisingly graceful. Since
> uniting all the Sandwich Islands in 1810, he's
> been enacting laws of peace. He's kind to
> widows and children. He treated me as an

equal, which says a lot about a monarch. Being the ship's cooper, I promised to make him barrels for storing some of his wealth. By the grace of the Almighty, I made it off the ship and to Maui with my own small barrel and store of wealth.

This is wonderful! I'm not only holding history in my hands, Abby thought, *but a mystery as well!* Who was this sailor, and what happened to him after his ship was lost? Though she wanted to read straight through, she grew sleepy. How long had it been since she'd had a good night's sleep? She lay down on the bunk and pulled a blanket around her shoulders. That night she dreamt of a tall king who was kind to a widow. . . .

When Abby woke the next morning, the porthole in her cabin showed gray light just breaking. She eagerly opened the diary and picked up where she'd left off the night before. She couldn't wait to discover what happened to the barrel maker, the ship's cooper. It didn't take long for her to learn that he'd been befriended by the island king, who invited him to live in the red-brick palace he'd built for his queen, Kaahumanu. The king was eager to learn all he could about England and America, places the cooper had been. Eventually, as Abby read on, she could see he had become one of the king's confidants. He was given land and *kanaka* workers to clear and plant it so he could stay on Maui even after the king returned to his permanent home. But while the king was in residence on Maui, the cooper was expected to stay close by his side. The journal recorded this clearly:

April 1815—Kamehameha has a heart as big as his shoulders, but the island king fully trusts no one but his favorite queen, Kaahumanu. There are moments when he does not trust her completely, either! I've seen them argue something fierce, both of them people of huge passions. And it's said that long ago, she took another lover and, when he discovered it, he chased after her with a club. But she made it to the "city of refuge," where a *kapu*-breaker is safe. Eventually she was forgiven. Aye, 'tis common knowledge that he loves her more than himself. These people are good people, full of love and easy laughter. Now that the king has brought an end to interisland wars, they are a peaceful people as well.

But still, he does not trust even the men he has surrounded himself with. We must all stay close by; p'rhaps he fears we will attempt an overthrow of his government. . . .

In one thing he does have reason to mistrust me: Though I never thought I could love again, I have in this past year fallen in love with his adopted daughter, the Princess Kalele. She returns my love and vows to never wed the chief which her adopted father, King Kamehameha, has chosen for her. He is a chief of much power on Kauai. My Kalele will stay here when the king and his entourage departs, for she will be preparing for her wedding. Soon she will be sent off to her betrothed if I do not come up with a plan. . . . I am desperate these nights, pacing my floor in the king's red-brick palace.

I would give all my riches for her. She already owns my heart.

Abby's eyes grew moist with emotion as she read his desperate words. She was dying to know what became of the two star-crossed lovers, but the ship's bell had just rung, calling her to breakfast.

After sitting out on deck with the boys and Duncan for an hour, filling them in on the diary, Abby headed back to her cabin to read. She just *had* to know how the story ended! Her heart raced as she read on:

Kalele was sent off in the night to Kauai; the king must have suspected her feelings for me. I

186

am making plans to follow right away. Then
we will use my gold to charter a ship to California. . . . Hopefully, she will consent to sail
farther. Someday soon, I may even see my
family again. How I miss my child. . . .

The cooper also recorded thoughts of his life in his
village back home, where his brothers and sisters
lived. The day flew by for Abby as she read the diary
almost to the end. Not long afterward, she heard a
sailor topside shout out, "Land ho!"

They had arrived in Kailua, and it was mid-
afternoon. She was almost home, but she couldn't
help wondering what was going to happen to Luke.
Would Duncan force him to go back to California?
She was afraid to ask, but in a few hours she'd know
the answer one way or the other.

Chapter Twenty-One

After being rowed ashore, Abby and her party visited Olani. The royal chieftess insisted Abby again ride Sugar home. "You be my *nani*-hair," Olani insisted. "We be sisters of the heart. And you will send Sugar home with this Duncan man." Abby hugged the chieftess with pleasure and agreed she would.

"I need to make one stop before we head home," Abby announced as she led them to the small mercantile. "*Aloha*, Kipini!" she said brightly as she entered the store.

The gentle Hawaiian *wahine* loaded many green apples, cornmeal, eggs, and dried jerky into a basket. "We'll take some ribbon candy, too," Luke said eagerly. As Kipini piled six lengths of hard confection onto a banana leaf, Luke shook his head. "More," he urged.

Kipini looked mutely at Abby, who nodded. She added another ten pieces to the pile. Abby joyfully handed her a silver coin from the bag, and they headed out into the sunlight.

"Before we get sick on candy," Duncan commented, "let's have some apples." He pulled out a silver dirk from his belt sheath and cut two apples horizontally.

Abby was astonished. "Why—you cut apples just like my Uncle Samuel!"

Duncan grinned. "I like to see the starrr, lassie." He handed her a juicy piece.

She bit into it and remembered what her uncle had taught. "Uncle Samuel says everyone has special talents hidden inside, just like that star."

Duncan considered Abby's words, then dipped his large blunt finger into the apple core and extracted seeds. Solemnly he handed a tiny seed to Abby.

"Miss Abigail, let this seed rrremind ye that hidden in ye is the mighty talent o'loving others. . . . and may it also remind ye to listen better to God's voice o'direction." Abby blushed as she hid the seed in her palm.

Duncan handed another seed to Kini. "Kini, the talent within ye is courage. By brrravery, ye set yer friends free. Now may God add knowledge to yer valor." The young boy's face glowed with the compliment as he tucked the apple seed into his pouch.

Duncan paused, his steel gray eye probing Luke. "Luke, ye possess the grrreat gift of loyalty."

Duncan gazed down at the little seed Luke took from his fingertip. "Hidden in this seed," he continued, "is the power of new life. May God sprout new life in ye and . . . courage, the courage to forgive."

Abby was stunned.

Duncan reached out a beefy paw and clapped Luke's shoulder. "Yer a lad I'd be proud to call me own son."

Luke's face was curtained by hair as he looked down, scuffing the dirt. When he met Duncan's gaze, Abby drew in a sharp breath. She'd rarely seen his green eyes so luminous with emotion. Duncan had struck a chord. His words had gone straight to Luke's heart.

Kini broke the mood. "Abby, it is true ribbon candy taste more better than *poi?*"

Luke threw back his head and belly laughed. "After one taste, Kini, you might never eat *poi* again!" They started up the hill that led out of town.

Hoping to arrive at Uncle Samuel's ranch before nightfall, they pressed on hurriedly. Duncan and Luke walked alongside Sugar, who bore Abby and Kini. After two hours of hiking, they stopped for a short break. Kini and Luke lay down in the shade of a kukui grove that ran along a stream, while

Duncan retrieved from the saddlebags the lunch Olani had provided.

Since Luke and Kini had fallen asleep, Duncan sliced off a thick piece of brown bread and a hunk of cheese for both Abby and himself. They walked toward the creek a few yards away and sat on a rock to enjoy their late lunch. A red bird flitted on the branch of a plumeria tree and cocked its head toward them. Abby and Duncan sat listening to the music of the brook, which gurgled and tripped over its shallow bed. Abby bowed her head and prayed silently, then folded the bread over the cheese and took a bite. Duncan did the same.

After a bit he spoke up. "If I've figured corrrectly, lassie, we could make yer uncle's ranch before the moon gets too high tonight." He took another bite and winked at her.

She smiled. Duncan was a good man, a caring man deep inside. If only he could understand Luke's plight. "Duncan, I know you were hired by Mrs. Gronen to bring Luke back, but there are some things you don't know. . . . She, she's been unkind to him."

Duncan stopped eating, too. His forefinger and thumb crept up to his moustache and twirled the handlebar absently. "I could see she was a harrrd woman, Abby. And I know, too, that Luke has suffered much. Like meself, he's lost both his dear parents. There be nothing harder for a young lad to endure." Duncan gazed down at the stream. "But what can I do? I've accepted the job."

"Could you take some gold from me and return her money?" Abby asked hopefully.

"Lassie, it's not that I *want* to brrring the lad back to her . . . it's that I've already said I'd do it. I've given me word." He sighed heavily, the food forgotten.

Abby hung her head and squeezed the life out of her bread and cheese. She wasn't hungry anymore. *It shouldn't be this way!* God had done so much for her, but she desperately ached to have Luke belong to her family . . . forever.

Abby stood up to leave when Luke suddenly appeared. "It's all right, Ab. I've . . . I've decided to go back with Duncan."

Abby's face paled. "Why?" she croaked.

"I think it's what God wants," Luke said slowly. "I don't know God very well, but . . . that's my own fault. I haven't given Him much of a chance. Maybe this is His way of helping me learn about Him. . . . I mean, Duncan knows a lot. Don't you?" he asked, turning toward the Scotsman.

"I'd be happy to share what I know, Luke. And I'm imprrressed with yer decision. Ye sound like a man."

Kini woke then and stumbled over to the group. "Where did food go?"

"Here," Abby said, holding out her squashed bread and cheese.

Kini looked at it and grinned. "New food?" he asked, eager to try the *haole* way of eating.

"You can call it 'Smashed Sandwich,' " Abby said.

"Mmmmm . . ." Kini had no complaints, and everyone laughed as he ate it quickly and scouted around for more.

Duncan handed him his leftovers. "Yer a grrrowing lad, Kini." He brushed the crumbs from his moustache. "Now, Luke, what do ye say we get Abby and Kini safely home?"

"I say it's the right thing to do, Duncan." The two of them shook on it. As Abby watched, an unspoken message passed across their locked hands, from Luke's green eyes to Duncan's unpatched eye. Peace settled over Abby, surprising her. *Could this be God's plan for Luke . . . to bring him a step closer . . . to his true home?*

Then Luke took a huge hunk of bread and cheese and dug in. Kini imitated him, and the two happily munched away. When it was time to leave, Kini said he wanted to walk aways, so Luke stepped up into Sugar's saddle and gave Abby a hand up behind him. "It's a good way to spend time together before I go," Luke said.

A lump rose in Abby's throat. She was glad Luke sat in front of her and couldn't see how teary her eyes had become. She wrapped her arms tightly around his waist so she wouldn't slip backwards as Sugar started the long climb up the mountain.

Laying her head against Luke's warm back, Abby spoke so only he could hear. "Luke, I can't believe I'm saying this, but I think you made the right choice. You know I'll pray for you every day, but . . ." Her tongue felt too thick to speak. "I'll miss you something fierce."

Luke turned his head and saw the tears in Abby's eyes. "I love you, Ab."

"I know," she said, trying to swallow. "I love you, too!"

A short while later, Abby took the cooper's diary from her satchel and began to read where she'd left off. Since Kini and Duncan walked, they traveled slowly. This gave Abby three more hours to read. She was so engrossed in the unfolding events that she strained her eyes to see as the light grew dim. But she couldn't bear to quit, for she was beginning to put pieces of the puzzle together. At last she came to a page that almost stopped her breathing:

> I've met a James Canter, whose ship, *Beauty,* is at my disposal. I've promised him a share of my gold, and he's promised to help me get to Kauai and escape from there with my princess. Granted, he is an unsavory sort, but harmless, I think. Indeed, I haven't much choice for there are but seven ships at anchor off Lahaina—and every one of their captains is a friend of the king.

With a start Abby realized it must be the same Captain Jim who had thrown them overboard near Lanai. Yes, he'd said he'd been in the islands for many years. . . . And he was the captain of the *Beauty*. Though the darkness made it hard to see the words, Abby brought the diary close to her face and squinted.

She continued to read on, intrigued by the unfolding events. Soon, however, it was almost hopeless. The fine handwriting was too small to read in the dim light. Abby flipped to the last page and discovered that the scroll was much larger there. The writing looked like a last will and testament.

She made out a few words, then gasped. It was too incredible to be true, and yet the pieces fit! Luke had turned in the saddle at the sound of her surprise. "What's wrong?"

"The gold . . . it's not mine!"

Abby held up the diary with a trembling hand. "It's all in here."

Luke reined in Sugar to a stop, and Abby slid off. She fixed her gaze on Duncan. "The cooper made it to Kauai and married his princess in a secret ceremony. But she didn't want to leave the islands. She believed she could convince the king to accept their marriage.

"She needed time to do that, but two nights later she got word that a plot was hatching on Kauai to have the cooper murdered. So she hurried him to the *Beauty*, promising to have word sent to a secret spot on Lanai when the king approved their marriage and he could return."

Duncan looked fascinated. Abby pushed her curls back from her face and rushed on. "The *Beauty* took him to the secret rendezvous on Lanai, but the cooper began to mistrust the captain. The man, Jim Canter, was greedy." She eyed Luke. "It was Captain Jim! The same devil who threw us overboard! He wanted more gold than he originally agreed to, and the cooper was angry about his treachery. Abby paused, finding the next words hard to say. "He suspected the captain might not only be greedy but might murder him for the gold. There were others who wanted him dead as well.

"So he went ashore that night and hid his journal and some gold and silver coins in a money bag in the banyan tree. Right before, he made a map and a copy of his last will and testament for Kalele. He wrote her a letter, telling her about the treasure on Lanai . . . in case he didn't make it back to her. In his journal, he wrote that he would secretly pay the cabin boy two gold pieces to deliver the papers to her. Obviously, the map never made it to Kalele because it fell into Jackal's hands. It's the same map I took from him when he mutined on Captain Chandler's ship."

Abby flipped the pages of the diary until she found what she was looking for. "In one of his last entries, he writes about how much he loves the princess. He talks about his plans to hide his money, make the map, and send the letter to Kalele.

This letter has in it the name and address of his only child, whom he also loves. He wants her to find his child and deliver something. . . ."

Abby turned to the last page, her hands shaking. "The letter would have contained a copy of this— his last will and testament."

Abby looked away from Duncan, whose face had gone suddenly white. The atmosphere had grown electric. As Abby began to read the last will and testament, the hair on her arms stood up.

"I, Ian Argyle MacIndou, being of sound mind and body, do hereby bequeath all my worldly possessions to my only son, of Glasgow, Scotland— Duncan Stuart MacIndou." She raised her head to Duncan. "That's you, isn't it, Duncan?"

Duncan took a steadying breath and held his hand out for the diary. He stared for a long minute at the writing. His eyes brimmed and his face grew tight. "I've been looking me whole life for me father, and then ye find him for me here in the Sandwich Isles. . . . I . . . I cannot believe it! But ye've done it, lassie!" He enfolded her in a bear hug.

"But Duncan, don't you see? That means the gold is yours."

"Ah, yes . . . the gold." He nodded. The last rays of sun struck his dark hair and moustache, laying on him like a golden mantle.

It seemed a weight had fallen from Duncan as he squared his shoulders. "With every job I had as a prrrivate investigator, whether I was out to catch a crook or find a lost family member, I expected pay. Ye, Abby, deserve a good deal fer helping me discover what happened to me father. I will split the gold with ye: fifty-fifty."

Abby gasped. "Truly?"

"Aye, lassie. 'Tis well deserved."

Abby grinned at Luke and Kini. "I still have a treasure to bring Pa! It must be God's plan to provide for us. Don't you think?" she questioned Luke.

"Yep, it's bound to be just enough for what lies ahead. If there's one thing I keep learning, Abby," Luke said, "it's that God's here for us." Then he reached deeply into his pants' pocket and extracted his rabbit's foot. "This hasn't been that lucky after all," he said as he swung it around over his head and released it. The foot flashed white as it went flying over a stand of ferns.

"Why, Luke," Abby said, her eyes round with wonder.

Kini shook his head. "*Haole* be funny people! Girl and boy eat together. They have feet of rabbit that fly through air."

Everyone laughed as joy washed over the group. "Let's press on," Abby said. "We're almost home. Duncan, when you came here looking for Luke, did my pa seem perturbed that we'd left home without his permission?"

Duncan twirled his moustache while he carefully considered his answer. "*Perturbed* isn't the right word, Abby."

"Oh, dear."

Luke gave her a hand to get up onto Sugar's back. He suppressed a smile. "Ah, Duncan and I will be heading on to Aunt Dagmar's now. I have a feeling I'll live longer if I go directly to California and face *that* dragon."

"Oh, no, you don't! We're going into the lion's den together. But Kini, don't you worry. Pa will be pleased as sassafras to meet the brave boy who rescued his daughter. Even . . . even if that daughter has to go cut a switch for herself as soon as she arrives," Abby said, grimacing.

Duncan chuckled. "I wouldn't worry, lassie. What comes to mind when I think o'yer pa is a man full o'worry and love fer ye." Then he sobered and tightened his grip on the diary. "I misjudged me own pa, thinking he'd forgotten me. But this journal proves I was never far from his mind. And if a human pa can love that much—lads and lassie—yer Father in heaven is ever thinking o'ye."

Then the one-eyed Scotsman winked fondly at them and broke into a Welsh hymn. Abby's heart soared with hope as the tune carried them home.

> *Which of you, if his son asks for bread, will give him a stone? Or if he asks for a fish, will give him a snake? If you, then, though you are evil, know how to give good gifts to your children, how much more will your Father in heaven give good gifts to those who ask him!*
>
> Matthew 7:9-11

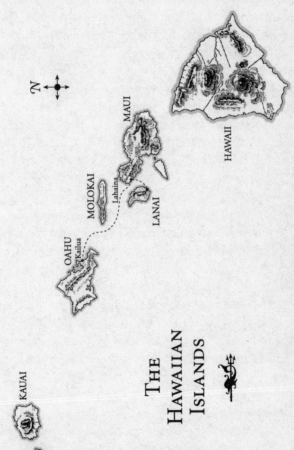

THE
HAWAIIAN ISLANDS

N

KAUAI

OAHU
Kailua

MOLOKAI

Lahaina

LANAI

MAUI

HAWAII

*Don't miss the next exciting adventure in
the South Seas Adventures series:*

Abby
California
Gold

What happens when Abby and Sarah's ma gets
sick and they must sail back to California with
Kini, Luke, and Duncan? Will they, like the
other Californios, catch gold fever? You'll have
to read it to find out!

Hawaiian People, Places, and Words

Follow these two simple rules to say Hawaiian words correctly:

1. Don't end a syllable with a consonant. For example, Honolulu should be pronounced Ho-no-lu-lu, not Hon-o-lu-lu.

2. Say each vowel in a word. The vowels generally are pronounced like this:
   a as in daughter
   e as in prey
   i as in ring
   o as in cold
   oo as in tool

ali'i—Hawaiian chief

aloha—word of welcome or farewell, a type of unconditional love shared

Great Mahele—land division meant to distribute the king's land among commoners and royalty

haole—white foreigner, usually a Caucasian

Kaahumanu—King Kamehameha's favorite wife, who served as Queen Regent after his death

kahuna—a priest of the Hawaiian religion, or a holy or wise man

kahuna nui—head of the village

kamali'i—children

King Kamehameha—the great king who united all the islands and brought peace

kanaka—Hawaiian man or worker (also men)

kane—man or male

kapu—something that is taboo or off limits

Kauai—the northernmost of the large islands in the chain

keiki—child

Lanai—small island near Maui and Molokai

nani wahine—pretty girl

mahalo—thank you

makai—to the beach

malo—loincloth

mana—shadow

Maui—A large island, home of Lahaina, the whaling capital of the Pacific

mauka—toward the mountains

Molokai—one of the three islands that form a natural triangle (with Maui and Lanai)

muumuu—Hawaiian dress

nui—big

Oahu—A large island in the chain, where Honolulu is located

pikake—small, very fragrant white flower used to make a lei

poi—a Hawaiian staple made from the taro plant

pu-pus—snack foods or hors d'oeuvres

tapa—cloth made from the bark of the paper mulberry tree

wahine—woman or female (also women)

Nautical Words

bow—front of ship

cooper—someone who makes barrels

duck cloth—a heavy fabric for work clothes

gunwale—the upper edge of a boat

jollyboat—skiff or rowboat used to take sailors from ship to shore

mast—wooden beam that holds up the sails

schooner—a sailing vessel with at least two masts

starboard—to the right, or right side

stern—back of ship

About the Author

Pamela Walls, a freelance reporter, sailed through Hawaii and fell in love with the islanders. "After my sailing job ended," Pamela says, "my girlfriends and I camped on a beach with a large Hawaiian family, who fed us *poi*. We'd run out of food, and they were generous—although one helping of *poi* was definitely enough.

"Every year this family brought their refrigerators and generators to the beach for a six-month camp out. The grandparents rose at dawn and took the kids swimming in the ocean, and the parents got up and went to work! At night everyone swam again, went fishing (with nets), and cooked dinner together."

While in Hawaii, Pamela went deep-sea fishing and caught a forty-five-pound ono; swam with a deadly, venomous sea snake (not on purpose!); and loved chasing green sea turtles underwater. "But seeing humpback whales spy-hop was definitely a highlight," she says. Spy-hopping is when a whale "stands up" out of the sea and stares into the faces of sailors onboard a ship.

"These gentle giants appear as curious about us as we are about them," Pamela says. "Once I was a mile offshore in a rubber inflatable boat when a whale swam under our Zodiac. I put on a face mask and dunked my head underwater to catch a glimpse. With his pectoral fins stretched out, that fifty-foot whale looked like a 747 jet. But he turned his body so one eye could stare up at me. His gray eye reflected an intelligence, and we gazed at each other for one awe-inspiring minute! His twelve-foot tail fluke, which was undulating up and down, was about to hit me in the face. Suddenly he stopped swimming—allowing himself to sink—and our boat passed over him.

"I hope the Abby books share some of the wonder and joy I've found in God's creatures. Living in Hawaii helped me realize our Creator is a genius. And don't even get me started on the beautiful sunsets!"

> *How many are your works, O Lord! In wisdom you made them all; the earth is full of your creatures. There is the sea, vast and spacious, teeming with creatures beyond number—living things both large and small. There the ships go to and fro, and the leviathan, which you formed to frolic there.*
>
> Psalm 104:24-26